MW01166985

BAJA MALIBU
and Other Stories

BAJA MALIBU
and Other Stories

Robert Bradford

GO WEST PRESS
2015

BAJA MALIBU and Other Stories

Robert Bradford

© Robert Bradford, 2015

All rights reserved. No part of this publication may be reproduced, stored in a retrieval system, or transmitted, in any form or by any means—electronic, mechanical, by photocopying, recording or otherwise—without the prior permission of Robert Bradford, except for brief quotations in reviews and scholarly publications.

ISBN: 978-0-578-16239-3
Softcover

Go West Press
www.gowestpress.com

This is a work of fiction. Names, characters, businesses, places, events and incidents are either the products of the author's imagination or used in a fictitious manner. Any resemblance to actual persons, living or dead, or actual events is purely coincidental.

Book design and type formatting by Susan Blettel

Dedicated to Ann,
Hank and Allee

"We live as we dream — alone..."

—Joseph Conrad, *Heart of Darkness*

PREFACE

EACH TIME YOU CROSS THE BORDER, you just don't know what's going to happen. You drive through a bright green light and there's the first sniff test—a kid no older than twenty with camo two sizes too big for him and an M-16 slung over his shoulder motions for you to stop.

You smile, take your sunglasses off so he can see your friendly blue eyes and get out of the car. The kid opens the doors, looks at your surfboards, smells your dank wetsuits and nods his head.

"Ten un buen dia," he says.

"Igualmente."

Easy enough. Now you follow the signs to the *playas* and crane your neck out the window in the hazy light before sunrise to see if there are any hints of surf. You can detect four-foot waves breaking on the reefs and you're feeling good about life.

The first check is Baja Malibu and you have high hopes that it's going to be firing. You ask the two fellas at the gate if you can park and take a look at the waves and they tell you, *"Por supuesto."* You've tipped them enough to where they recognize you. There's the walk down the funky cobblestone street to the lookout and the first disappointment. You thought Baja Malibu was going to be close to perfection, but the swell angle is just not right—it's walled up and there's a light south wind creating texture on the water that's somewhere between green and brown.

Back in the car and the hunt continues. You make your way to Campo Lopez, a hodgepodge of mobile homes in various hues of green and orange, modified Airstreams with add-on rooms and rough, hand-built houses that are a refreshing throwback to Mexico in the 1970s. You make your way down the trail to the beach and say hello to some old friends—two angry rottweilers that snarl, jump and let you know that if only they could get over their fence...

The walk is worth it. As you stand on the beach, A-frame peaks explode in front of you. The paddle out is not too bad and you trade waves with a friend, mindful every now and then between sets to look north to the headlands and south to the point where there are no houses, no pending developments, no signs of encroachment on the natural world. This is Mexico the way it's supposed to be—hell, this is life the way you want it to be. No responsibility. No crowds. No schedule. Maybe you can sell everything, buy a trailer in Campo Lopez and eat *carnitas* or *lengua* every day. It wouldn't be that hard to do, you tell yourself.

But life across the border calls you; a few hours later you're in the seemingly endless lineup in Tijuana and there's a familiar old man dressed in an ill-fitting white suit asking you to give money to his church to help the poor. You hand him a few pesos and he directs you to the quickest line across the border. There's a final sniff test with American Homeland Security agents. You smile for a stout woman with big arms and Ray-Bans who asks you what you have been doing. "Surfing. Nothing more," you tell her. She waves you through and now you're driving on the 805 through Chula Vista and there's something different about the American sky—it's somehow not as blue as it was just a few miles south.

THIS IS A BOOK ABOUT CROSSING BORDERS. The borders between countries, between cities, between people. It's a book about folks heading north and south, always looking for something better.

I remember seeing a television interview with Muddy Waters in the 1970s and he was talking about how he wished he could play guitar like the white kids who idolized him, like Duane Allman or Eric Clapton. They could play more notes than he could, Muddy said. And then I saw an interview with Eric Clapton saying how he just wished he could be like Muddy Waters, that above all else he wanted to sing or play just a few notes with that much soul. That's who we are—constantly searching to be someone else, never comfortable in our own skin.

San Diego is at its heart nothing more than a big border town. It's still what the essayist Edmund Wilson called in 1931 the Jumping-Off Place. It's a good place for someone like me, a place where you can, at a moment's notice, run for your life. South to a country that is at once violent and welcoming. North to the Hollywood of your dreams and youth. And west—always west—to the ocean that helps you make sense of the confused world around you.

TABLE OF CONTENTS

Shipwreck

IT'S A FUNNY THING about Americans abroad. They always seem to find each other. In the hundred miles of isolated beach and desert on the tip of Baja California, you run into the same American tourists and expats again and again. Whether you want to or not.

My buddy Gary and I go to San José Del Cabo every spring around Cinco de Mayo to surf and drink. It's a ritual for us, a chance to get rid of our wetsuits, surf in warm water and take advantage of the early south swells that hit southern Baja. We stay outside of San José, a nice little village that is about forty-five minutes and a world away from Cabo San Lucas. Any place where some idiot like Sammy Hagar is considered a hero is just not right. That's Cabo San Lucas. Cabo San Lucas is the kind of place where my fat friend who sells computers in the Silicon Valley goes with his fat wife for a Mexican experience. They sit around the Marriott pool like elephant seals, drink weak margaritas and get sunburned. At sundown, they go to the Cabo Wabo Cantina with scores of other sunburned American tourists hoping to see Sammy, who's rarely there, and drink more weak margaritas. Around midnight they waddle back to their room and try to get romantic and end up passing out. And they do the same thing the next night.

Gary and I stay at our good friend Harry Solomon's house on the East Cape, a rough thirty-minute drive on dirt roads from San José. Harry bought the house in the early 1970s when there were just a handful of expats on the entire East Cape. He tells stories about surfing perfect point breaks for weeks with no one out and you could drive for miles and only see wild burros and roadrunners and rattlesnakes. Now he's surrounded by expats and drug dealers who have built huge estates powered by industrial-grade generators. They throw wild parties with electric mariachi bands blasting until five in the morning.

But Harry is not leaving the East Cape. You see, he met a girl there about fifteen years ago at the beginning of the real estate boom. Melanie was in her early twenties then, a bright kid from Point Loma right out of San Diego State who grew up in a real estate family. She knew how to sell, had connections with good mortgage bankers and she was highly confident that the market in Cabo would catch on fire in a few years. She was right. She was driving around the East Cape looking at the simple bungalows with dollars in her eyes and she ran across Harry sitting under his *palapa* doing some work on one of his longboards. Even today, Harry is a handsome guy with thick, black wavy hair and what plastic surgeons call perfect facial structure. He was in his forties when he met Melanie—but still tan and lean.

"Do you live here year-round?" Melanie asked.

"Why do you want to know? And who the hell are you? I didn't know the locals were hiring blonde building inspectors with great asses to cruise around the Cape."

Harry didn't know that he was in over his head.

He offered to take Melanie to dinner in the village of San José, provided they didn't talk about real estate. They went to *Mi Cocina,* with its thirty-foot ceilings and the huge murals of Mexican landscapes on the walls. Harry did what he always does—he ordered Cadillac margaritas and steamed baby clams to start and the fresh grilled *dorado* and shrimp with a *molé* sauce. They danced to a real mariachi band until the place closed and Harry drove them home half drunk on the dirt road to the cape, barely missing mule deer that appeared like gray phantoms, their eyes shining in the headlights of his old Blazer.

When they got to the bungalow, Harry told me later, Melanie jumped out of the truck, immediately pulled her dress over her head and skipped to the porch. Harry fucked her there the first time and they worked their way around every room in the bungalow for the rest of the night. They woke up hungover on the front porch, covered by a Mexican blanket that Harry haggled for on *Boulevard Mijares*. The morning light was warm and they could see gray whales breeching offshore.

Harry was ruined after that first night with Melanie. A week later he returned to Leucadia and his wife, Jenny, who was twenty years older than Melanie and not nearly as sexually inventive. He immediately started planning his next surf trip to the East Cape. And he has been making excuses to go to San José as often as he can ever since.

GARY AND I GOT TO HARRY'S PLACE around one in the afternoon. There were cold Bohemias in the refrigerator—that was Harry's favorite beer and we have become converts. It was one of those rare afternoons with no wind and we quickly threw our boards and some beer in the rental minivan and headed to Shipwreck.

We got out of the car at the lookout over Shipwreck, which is named for some drug runner's boat that hit the reef late one night in the 1960s. It was point break perfection—overhead rights opening up for 75 yards down the beach. We had that anxious, joyous feeling as we pulled on our rash guards and then we heard our old friend—Bummer Jaime. Jaime is a lunatic expat from Oceanside who thinks he owns Shipwreck. Like the vast majority of surfers, he's a creature of habit—Shipwreck is the only place that he surfs. And he lets everyone in the water know that this is his break, even the Mexican locals.

"Don't even fucking think about dropping in on me," Jaime said to some poor longboarder who didn't know what to make of him. "I'll fucking kill you if you paddle near me again."

Gary and I smiled at each other as we put on our fins. We're kneeboarders—a dying breed of mutant surfers who ride waves on our knees and live for late takeoffs and deep barrels. As we paddled out, Gary greeted Jaime. We've been tolerating his crazy antics for years.

"Bummer, good to see you. I see you're still making friends."

"Fucking halfmen. You stay out of my way, too."

"Shut the fuck up and surf, Jaime. I don't want any drama from you today. It's too good to hear your mindless commentary."

Jaime didn't like to see us. We're both bigger and meaner than he is and we don't put up with his shit. Jaime paddled to the far end of the lineup and waited for the next set. We saw lines on the horizon and started paddling outside. Jaime, greedy fool that he is, was intent on taking off on the first wave, but the longboarder that he had been jawing at had better position. As Gary and I slowly paddled over the first wave, we saw the longboarder take off and Jaime dropped in down the line, right on his head. They both fell off their boards, arms and legs flailing, and Jaime was screaming even before he hit the water.

"Fucking kook. You're dead."

Gary and I picked off waves three and four of the set, screaming down the line with huge smiles on our faces. As we kicked out, we could see Jaime and the longboarder inside. Jaime was out of his mind, screaming until his voice cracked.

"You motherfucker. You need to get out of the fucking water now and never come back here again."

"I live here, you fuckin' moron. And I'll tell you something, I'm not goin' anywhere."

It was the first time we heard the longboarder talk, and we knew something wasn't right about him. He had a strong accent, maybe Oklahoma or Arkansas. He was in his late fifties, with a scraggly beard and one of those goofy surf hats that covered his gray hair. He was rail thin and short—it was clear that he was physically outmatched by Jaime.

Jaime jumped off his board and the water was shallow enough where he could stand. He slogged over to the longboarder, who threw one weak punch that glanced off Jaime's head, and then Jaime had him in a headlock. Gary and I looked at each other and we knew that we couldn't let Jaime choke the poor guy out. We paddled toward the mayhem and I got off my board and proceeded to get behind Jaime and put a headlock on him so he would release the longboarder. My plan worked, but when Jaime let go, the worthless prick elbowed me hard in the ribs with his free arm. I didn't want to hurt Jaime, but that pissed me off. I hit him hard three times in his left ear and he howled. Surfers tend to get a condition called exostosis. After years in the water, bone grows in your ear canal and it makes you prone to infections and you have pretty persistent pain. After Jaime started screaming, I concluded that he had a pretty good case of exostosis. He didn't elbow me anymore and I loosened my headlock on him.

"Jaime, what the fuck is wrong with you? Why do you have to go and beat up on some old longboarder? You need to get out of the water and chill for a while."

Jaime was holding his left ear and he looked like a beaten man. "Fuck you, halfman." I knew that he didn't have any fight left in him and he would do what I told him for once. Gary and I paddled back to the lineup and caught more waves for a good two hours. One of the Mexican locals, a heavyset guy with a mustache who looked like he could be a *Federale*, smiled at me. The locals liked to see Jaime get his ass kicked every now and then. They knew it wouldn't change him, but at least they didn't have to listen to him for the rest of the afternoon.

When we got back to the beach, the longboarder was sitting on a towel. He pulled his knees tight to his chest and you could see his spindly legs.

"I want to thank you fellas for helpin' me out. You got me out of a jam and I really 'ppreciate it. I just had back surgery and this was my first time back in the water. I learned that I still ain't got fuckin' nothin' out there."

"No problem, man. Bummer is a fucking lunatic. You have to watch him and put him in his place occasionally. You look familiar. Don't you surf at Destiladeras?"

"You bet. I've been surfin' that place since I moved here five years ago. Nice fellas that surf there. Not like this prick, Jaime."

"It's a fun break with a big swell."

"Sure is. Kind of reminds me of Rincon on a real good day."

"You've surfed Rincon a lot?"

"I moved to Ventura from Corpus Christi around '73. Coming from Texas, where the surf is only real good a couple of times a year if you're lucky, I was in heaven. I surfed Rincon, C Street, Hollywood by the Sea and even got on the Ranch every now and then. When there wasn't swell, we'd go surf fishing at Oxnard and catch barred perch and occasionally a halibut. We'd fill up a gunny sack with those perch and then we'd buy fresh strawberries and lima beans from the fruit stands. We'd throw huge parties, and I was always the cook. Bein' from Texas, I know how to fry fish and I would make a huge pot of lima beans with fatback. The girls would be walkin' around in their orange bikinis eatin' those strawberries and drinkin' tequila sunrises. They weren't as fine as Texas girls, but make no mistake, they were fine. Then we'd break out the Thai stick and everything would be good in the world."

He stood up to stretch and I could see a prominent keloid on his chest, about four inches above his heart. It had that bubble gum pink color and I couldn't help but stare at it.

"You like the look of that scar? I got that about a year ago. I was up north campin' just south of *Salsipuedes*. I had a nice four-wheel drive F-150 pickup that I fixed up. Raised with a primo camper shell. I was showin' too much money and I didn't know that gangs of meth heads were patrollin' the area. They pulled me out of the camper in the middle of the night, kicked the shit out of me, shot me and stole my fuckin' truck. But I'm all right right now. My name is Steve, by the way. Do you fellas want to come to my place and have a drink?"

WE FOLLOWED STEVE and navigated the narrow road that leads you out of Shipwreck. There were random crosses adorned with dead flowers along the ridge, signs of people who went too fast and ended up on the rocks below. Steve drove the perfect Cabo vehicle—a factory blue 1970 Ford Bronco with off-road tires and the removable top. He pulled into an impressive compound about ten minutes north of Shipwreck. There was a main house and a guest house—I'd estimate that he had about nine-thousand square feet of living space. He pulled into a garage that had a vintage Lincoln Continental, the model with the coffin doors. It was stock and immaculate. He was clearly a Ford man.

We sat in a huge open room with this broad view of the East Cape and Steve brought us Negra Modelos and we each had a shot of nice reposado tequila. I have a problem with being way too honest and direct. I can't help myself.

"So Steve, what the fuck do you do to live like this? Real estate? Drug dealer? Car mechanic?"

"I kind of got lucky. My old man was in the oil business in Houston. When that first fuckin' Bush, George Herbert Walker, came to Houston from Connecticut in the 1950s, my old man showed him the ropes. The Yankee didn't know shit about oil or barbecue or Texas. But my old man took care of him and he was grateful to my old man. My dad died of emphysema when I was living in Ventura and he made good provisions for all of us in his will."

"So what you're telling me is that you don't work and have been living large since the 1970s."

"That's about right."

"You're my fucking hero."

We drank more beers and shots and Steve made guacamole—he was a superb host and a good guy. We talked about perfect days at Nine Palms and Zippers and told our hero stories about the waves we made. Around dusk we heard a car pull up. The front door opened and in walked Melanie, wearing a lime green halter top that highlighted her still perfect breasts. She looked at me and Gary, surprised just for a moment, walked nonchalantly to the refrigerator and grabbed a beer.

"Hey Gary, hey Cole. What are you guys doing here?"

Steve walked up to Melanie, kissed her softly and slid his hand across her ass.

"Hey doll, do you know these fellas? They pretty much saved my life at Shipwreck today."

"We met Melanie years ago when we were thinking about buying a bungalow down here. Before the big places got built and real estate went insane."

"You should have bought then, Cole. I told you that this place was going to take off."

I looked at Gary while Steve, who was half drunk, played grab ass with Melanie. Gary shook his head and we both threw down shots.

"So how did the two of you meet?" I asked. I had already established myself as the blunt guy. I had nothing to lose.

"So I was changin' the oil on the Bronco one afternoon and I hear a car pull up. I'm under the truck right in the middle of the oil change and I don't want to be distracted. I hear the sound of flip-flops coming toward me and then I see these two beautiful brown legs. I slide out from under the Bronco and I get a peak underneath Melanie's dress. Hell, I thought I saw a little bit of heaven, fellas.

"Melanie introduced herself and wanted to know if I was interested in sellin' this place. She said she had a potential buyer for what she called a substantial place on the East Cape. I told her that we'd need to discuss the prospects more over a margarita."

"Thanks, Steve. A little too much on the details, but that is pretty much the way it happened," Melanie said.

"We've been together for comin' up on six months now. She's not from Texas, but I have learned to tolerate her."

We drank more shots and Steve broke out his collection of music. We listened to Doug Sahm and Bob Wills and Gatemouth Brown well into the night and any initial animosity I had toward Melanie slowly passed as I listened to her laugh and watched her and Steve try to two-step to "Faded Love."

GARY AND I MADE OUR WAY BACK TO HARRY'S around four in the morning. We could see eyes in the headlights, and I hoped that I wouldn't hit one of the mangy Mexican steers that carelessly walked the road in the night. I was so drunk that I drove with one eye closed.

"What the fuck are we going to tell Harry?" Gary asked.

"We can't tell him shit. It would kill him."

"I guess you're right."

What the fuck could you tell Harry? That the woman he lived for was banging some rich guy from Corpus Christi who, when all was said and done, was a pretty decent sort. And could you really blame Melanie? She couldn't just wait for Harry to come down every couple of months and entertain herself with a vibrator during the down times.

I wished that I wouldn't have seen any of them—Jaime or Steve or Melanie. I wished that Gary and I could have driven up to perfect, solitary Shipwreck with no one out and caught waves until our arms were jelly. And then we'd sit on an empty beach and drink Bohemias and take a nap and wake up and paddle out again. That was supposed to be the point of Mexico. That's why you traveled close to a thousand miles and drove down pocked dirt roads in the middle of the night. Not for recognition. For a moment of amnesia.

Ponto

PEDRO FUENTES WALKED ON PONTO JETTY with a Shakespeare rod and reel that he had fished with for thirty years in one hand and a five-gallon plastic bucket that held his tackle in the other. He walked steadily to the end of the jetty, looking to find a spot among his friends. Well behind him, his twelve-year-old grandson Dylan Fuentes tried to keep up.

"Wait for me, Poppy," Dylan said.

Pedro did not look back at the boy. Dylan's face was red, and he was sweating. He was about five feet tall and already he weighed close to one-hundred fifty pounds. He wore long gray shorts and black Vans with white socks pulled up almost to his knees. To complete the uniform, he had a white T-shirt and a red and black flannel shirt to keep him warm. It was late October, and a stiff offshore wind was blowing.

Pedro picked a spot at the end of the jetty next to his old friend, José Aguilar. He and José fished together at least three times a week.

"Hola, José. Como estas?"

"Asi, asi. No hay pescado esta mañana."

Dylan lumbered to the end of the jetty. "Good morning, Dylan," José said. "You need to bring us some luck."

After work and on weekends, Pedro met his friends at Ponto Jetty. The men who fished Ponto consistently were like family to Pedro. There was José, who was by far the best fisherman in the group. He made long, powerful casts with his ten-foot Daiwa surf rod and caught halibut, calicos, sculpin, bonito and barracuda. There was Juan Rulfo, whom Pedro would occasionally see at jobs. Juan was an artist with stucco and dry wall and he could use the thin blade of a trowel to effortlessly create any texture his clients desired. There was Fernando Delgado, a large, dark Dominican who cared more about drinking Tecate and talking about women than fishing.

Every now and then on a Saturday, when Dylan did not have plans to play video games with his friends, Pedro would pick the boy up in his beaten up gray Dodge Caravan and take him to Ponto. In October the beach was largely empty, although there was always a pack of surfers on Saturday bobbing off the end of the jetty when there was a swell from the south or northwest.

As Dylan stood with the men at the end of the jetty, Pedro told the boy to watch and learn from José as he made a cast into the set lines. Dylan saw the old man take two long steps and it looked like he was going to walk off the jetty as the momentum of his two-hand cast carried his body forward. But he stopped on the last rock, his back bent and his hands and rod pointing southwest to the surf.

"If I catch a halibut, I will let you reel it in, Dylan," José said.

"I hope you catch a big halibut and then we can grill it and make fish tacos," Dylan said.

In Spanish, Pedro spoke to José.

"The boy is always thinking about eating," Pedro said.

"He is almost as wide as he is tall," José said.

"Have you eaten the *carnitas* tacos at Flaco's?" Fernando asked. "They are the best in all of San Diego. And there are only women who work there. Have you seen the two sisters who run the place? One has a scar on her cheek and she looks like she has been in a knife fight. I would like to fuck both of those sisters."

"You know nothing about *carnitas,* Fernando. You are a fucking Dominican," Juan Rulfo said. "Now Lucia's, that is where they make the best *carnitas*. I come from Sonora and they understand *carnitas* there. You must have the right amount of fat and crunch for the perfect *carnitas*. That is what they understand at Lucia's. Have you seen the short woman at Lucia's who takes your order? One of the meanest bitches in all of San Diego. And she hates gringos. If the gringos take too long to order, she tells the cook to spit in their food. But I agree with you on the sisters at Flaco's. They are fine."

Pedro looked at Dylan to see if he had any understanding of the conversation.

Dylan spoke no Spanish, and this was a problem for Pedro. Pedro's son, Antonio, had married an Anglo girl named Mary Walters. They met at Oceanside High School and started dating during their junior year. Pedro understood why Antonio was attracted to Mary—she was short and compact, a dirty blonde with large breasts and a body that every teenage boy would want. Antonio was a linebacker on the football team, and he met Mary at a party after they both had a few beers. They drank shots of Southern Comfort and grappled in Antonio's Monte Carlo and were inseparable after that night. Whenever Mary came to the Fuentes house, she looked lost and frustrated when Pedro and his family occasionally spoke Spanish.

"Hola, María, bienvenidos. Como estás?" Pedro would say to Mary, trying to make her feel comfortable in his small home off Mission Avenue.

"Hello, Mr. Fuentes," Mary would reply. "My Spanish is not so good. But I'm doing fine."

"This is not a problem, Mary," Pedro said. "We can speak English only."

Still, Pedro was happy when Antonio and Mary were married a year after they graduated, and Antonio got a job with the phone company and Mary worked as an office manager for a small construction company. Mary became pregnant, and Pedro and his wife, Ana, were pleased. Antonio and Mary would come over to the Fuentes house on Sundays to watch the Chargers game and Ana would make *empanadas* and *tortas*. On a Sunday a few months before Dylan was born, Pedro was helping Ana in the kitchen when he heard Mary and Antonio talking in the living room.

"You know that our son is going to speak English only," Mary said. "There are too many illegals that can't speak English and look where they are. Cleaning houses or mowing lawns or digging ditches and taking jobs from people who were born here."

"Don't be so loud," Antonio said. "And don't say those things in front of my family."

PEDRO HAD COME TO THE UNITED STATES from Nayarit when he was fourteen, crossing the border at Nogales and making his way from the desert of Arizona to San Diego, where the Pacific Ocean was familiar to him. He got on with a construction crew and made friends with a stonemason, who taught him his trade. He met a girl from Jalisco—her name was Ana Mendez and she cleaned hotels in La Jolla and Del Mar. She was slightly built with large brown eyes, and Pedro would sometimes meet her after she finished her shift at the La Jolla Hotel and they would go to the cove and swim in the late evening until it got dark. They would ride in Pedro's pickup back to Oceanside and go to his tiny apartment and make love and smell the lingering sand and saltwater and think of the place where they grew up.

"The water has more colors in Nayarit, different shades of blue and turquoise," Pedro said.

"And it is so much warmer. I am always a little cold when I swim in the water here, even in the summer," Ana said.

"Are you cold now?" Pedro said.

"No, I am not cold, now, Pedro."

"And we can swim in the cove tomorrow and come back here again?"

"Yes, every day we can swim in the cove as long as we come

back here where it is warm."

Ana and Pedro were married for thirty years, and then Ana started complaining about stomach problems. She went to her doctor in September, and he ordered a few tests and diagnosed her with pancreatic cancer. She died in December, a few days short of her fiftieth birthday.

Pedro was lost and broken after Ana died, and he had nowhere to go. He knew that Mary did not like him and she never made him feel welcome in their home in Vista. Pedro and Ana's daughter, Claudia, had moved to Houston to work as a bookkeeper for a landscaping company, and she asked Pedro to come to Houston and live close to her. But Pedro had no desire to go to Houston. It was too far from the ocean and he didn't like the smell of the bay in Galveston and the brown water there.

Pedro spent his days cutting flagstone and brick and Mexican tile to make opulent outdoor kitchens for rich people in Rancho Santa Fe and La Jolla. He came home and drank a Negra Modelo and thought about Dylan and how he could help him do more than sit around and watch football games with his father and get fat and live only in a world of television and video games. That was the problem with America, he thought. The people live too much in their rooms and houses. They do not spend enough time in the world. At night, he dreamed of Ana and swimming in the warm water of the Pacific and catching dorados and cooking them on the beach.

NOW HE WAS WITH HIS GRANDSON and they were in the world and this was a good Saturday.

"Dylan, come down here and help me catch a calico," Pedro said.

"All right, Poppy," Dylan said.

Pedro made a short cast to the south with an ancient green and yellow Hellbender. He could not count the number of calico bass that he had caught with this lure through the years. He retrieved three times, jerked the lure, and then retrieved two times. He reeled twice more and felt a strike. His rod bent and a good calico pulled hard against the current.

"Let me take the fish off, Poppy," Dylan said.

"Okay, Dylan. Get the pliers out of the tackle box," Pedro said.

Dylan grabbed a rusty pair of needle-noses and slowly made his way down the rocks to the side of the jetty. Pedro maneuvered the bass close to Dylan. He could see the bronze and black back of the fish and knew it was a good calico—five or six pounds.

"Grab the fish by the bottom of his lip and get the pliers right above where he is hooked," he told the boy.

Dylan grabbed the lip of the bass, but he struggled to get the hook out of his mouth. The calico looked as though it was bending in half as it used its powerful tail to get away from Dylan. And then a set wave that neither Pedro nor Dylan could see as they focused on the fish hit the jetty and Dylan let go of the fish and was in the water. Pedro dropped his rod and took two quick steps down the rocks and jumped in the ocean. Dylan was barely keeping his head above the surf when Pedro reached him.

"Help me, Poppy. Help me," the boy said.

"I have you boy," Pedro said. He could barely wrap both of his arms around Dylan.

"Don't let go of me, Poppy. Don't let go."

"I will never let go of you, Dylan."

Pedro looked up and he could see the next set coming. The first wave slammed him into the jetty and he could feel something break inside of him. He kicked his feet hard and he felt a rock and pushed off the jetty. They were clear of the jetty for a moment, and the next wave of the set hit them. Pedro's only concern was keeping himself in between the rocks and the boy. He felt his head hit the back of a flat rock and he saw a lightning bolt and he knew that he would need stitches. The only good thing, he thought, is that at least the waves are moving us closer to the beach. He looked up briefly and saw José, Juan and Fernando running down the jetty toward him, but they could not reach him. It was better that way. He was the only strong swimmer in the group and he did not want to see any of his friends drown.

"Poppy, I'm scared. I think we are going to die."

"*Tranquilo, Dylan, tranquilo.* Be calm, son."

There was one more wave in the set and then Pedro knew they would be in water shallow enough where they could walk to the shore. He held the boy as tightly as he could and he heard Dylan grunt as he squeezed him hard.

"One more wave and then we are going to be on the beach. I will never let go of you."

The third wave hit them and they rolled like rag dolls in the water. Pedro waited to feel the impact of the rock, but this time he hit the sand bottom and he was relieved.

"I thought we were going to die, Poppy," Dylan said. "I didn't know that you could swim so good."

"*Estas bien,mi nieto?* Are you well?" Pedro asked

"I'm okay, Poppy."

"Then everything is good," Pedro said.

Pedro and the boy rolled on the sand and then he was on his knees with his arms still around Dylan.

"Everything is good."

Hollywood by the Sea

CORY AND JOSEPH MADE THE SHARP TURN on Fourth Street and skated to the front of Lucia's. Cory kicked up his Zero Single Skull in one perfect motion and caught it with his left hand. Joseph was old school—he rode a gun that he made in wood shop, a four-foot rounded pin that he shaped like a 1970s Lightning Bolt he saw at the Longboard House.

They got in line at Lucia's—the crowd was not bad for a Saturday night. Ernestina was taking orders, and there were some Zonies in the front of the line.

"Broseph, you gotta listen to this shit," Cory told Joseph.

A stout sunburned woman with short, curly brown hair started firing questions at Ernestina.

"Now what exactly is on the chicken tostada?"

"Chicken...lattuce...tomatoes...sour cream."

"Can I get cheese on it?"

"Yes. Chicken tostada with cheese."

"And can you take off the sour cream?"

"Yes. Chicken tostada with cheese, no sour cream."

"And can I get it on a flour tortilla?"

"No. Only a corn tortilla."

"Well, okay then."

Cory knew that there was going to be trouble for the Zonie when she finished her order. He knew that Ernestina was going to give one of the cooks a simple nod and he was going to spit in the tostada.

When Cory got to the front of the line, he was all business.

"Bean, cheese and egg burrito. Small *horchata*."

"And you?" Ernestina asked Joseph.

"Carne asada burrito. Large root beer."

Ernestina never smiled, but Cory thought that their order might make her happy for a little while, until the next tourists got to her.

They sat outside on the picnic bench and watched the traffic go by on the 101. Young Asians revved trick Honda Civics that screamed like windup Hot Wheels. A lime green VW camper stalled at the stop sign in front of Lucia's, and Cory and Joseph got up and helped an old surfer push-start it. The surfer leaned against the car from the driver's side and steered with one hand, and they could see the crack of his ass as his board shorts slipped down. The camper sputtered and the dude jumped in the driver's seat and headed down the road. He didn't acknowledge the boys, and they walked back to their seat and Cory ate his burrito and some egg dropped on the bench.

"Brah, why do you get fucking egg on your burrito? You know you're going to fucking kill me later with those nasty farts," Joseph said.

"No worries, Broseph. We'll be so high you won't even care," Cory said.

They left Lucia's and skated to Stone Steps. They walked down the stairs to the beach, and Cory took off his backpack and got out a brown bag with a can of antique white spray paint. He shook it hard, the clicking of the can echoing off the cliffs and rising above the weak waves breaking on the beach. He opened the bag and made three long sprays in the bottom. He put the bag around his mouth and nose and breathed in, not too hard so he wouldn't get paint on his face. He handed the bag to Joseph, who huffed like a pro. A couple more sprays, a couple more huffs.

They sat against the cliff and looked out into the darkness. The paint hit them hard and fast. It's so much better than smoking a joint, Cory thought, as the first wave of the paint did what it was supposed to do. The paint killed the past and the future—it only permitted the dull, narcotic moment. They put their heads against the cliff, barely conscious, thinking about nothing and then they nodded. They woke up around one in the morning and slowly made their way up the stairs. Cory skated to Paradise Valley, a mobile home park full of tiny, two-bedroom trailers from the 1960s and 1970s. He quietly opened the door to his trailer and stumbled down the short hallway to his room. He passed out with his clothes on and he was awakened at about six in the morning by his mother, who pounded on his chest and head, her bony arms and fists flailing.

"Mom, what are you doing?"

"Get up, you little fucker. I need your help. You're never there for me and I need your help."

"What do you need?"

"I need you to do something for me for once. You never do anything for me."

"What do you want, Mom?"

"I'm fucking starved. I need something to eat. I need a doughnut and I need some coffee. I can't go out of the house. Look at me."

"Mom, stop hitting me and I'll get a doughnut for you."

The beating stopped, although Cory's mom couldn't really

hurt him. She was about five nine and weighed a little over ninety pounds. She had been a meth head since Cory was three, and Cory watched her get thinner and meaner and crazier every year. When he was little, he would find her stash and try to hide it from her. He learned early that you can't hide anything from a meth head—money, drugs, anything valuable. They can't reason, but they can find anything that they think will help them get high. They're like bloodhounds, he thought. His mom would look for hours to find meth. And she would always find it. So Cory gave up trying to hide things from her or helping her. He grabbed his flip-flops and headed to the door.

"I need some money, Mom."

"Here's two bucks. Get yourself a doughnut, if you want one."

Cory skated to Tommy's Donut Shop where Tommy and his wife Lonnie greeted him. They were from Korea.

"Hey Cory, how are you doing, man?" Tommy said. It was hard for Cory to hear Tommy try to talk like he was from California, but he was always nice to Cory and that meant something.

"Fine, Tommy. I need a bear claw, a sugar doughnut and a medium coffee, please."

"Cool." It sounded like *coor* to Cory. "Anything else, man?"

"No thanks, Tommy. How much will that cost? I only have two dollars."

"No problem, Cory. Two bucks will work."

He skated back to Paradise Valley and his mom was sitting on the couch with her eyes glazed and Cory could see her tiny pupils. He handed her the bag with the doughnut and the coffee, and she clawed open the bag and ate half the doughnut quickly.

"Is there any change or did you steal it?"

"No, Mom. No change. It was more than two bucks, but Tommy gave me a break."

"Those fucking chinks don't give anyone a break."

"Whatever, Mom."

He left her with her sugar and caffeine and went to see Joseph, who lived in an apartment complex a few blocks from Lucia's. Joseph was sitting on the balcony drinking a Dr Pepper. His mom had left for her job at Cole's Diner around four thirty and she wouldn't be home until after the lunch shift ended at three. Maybe. There was a good chance that she would go to the Derby for happy hour and start drinking rum and Cokes, and if she was lucky she'd pick up some guy who would pay for her drinks and go home with him. Cory and Joseph skated to the top of Stone Steps to check out the surf, and it was knee-high and closed out with wind on it.

"This has been the worst fucking summer ever," Cory said.

"Totally."

"We need to get the fuck out of here. Take a road trip."

"Where do you want to go?"

"North. Orange County. LA. Ventura. Santa Barbara. There's got to be something better than this shit."

"I heard that Hollywood by the Sea can get good in the summer. And my brother told me about this place called Jalama near Santa Barbara. Epic south swells."

"Let's go, Broseph. Today. Right fucking now."

"I'm there, dude."

They went to Joseph's apartment and got a backpack and he searched in his mom's dresser drawer for money and found eighteen dollars. Joseph strapped his twin-fin fish on the surf rack of his mountain bike and followed Cory to Paradise Valley.

"Wait here, Broseph. I'll be right out."

Cory's mom was passed out on the couch and she smacked her lips occasionally while she slept. Cory looked in her stash box for money and there was twelve dollars. He put a few T-shirts, some board shorts, a towel and a spring suit in his backpack. He grabbed his tri-fin thruster, potato chip thin, and he was good to go. He looked at his mother, one tiny breast coming out of her thrift shop Hawaiian shirt, muttered "Fuck you, bitch" and closed the door quietly.

CORY AND JOSEPH FELT GOOD riding on Highway 101. There was a slight south wind at their backs and the traffic was light. They rode past Ponto and there were already twenty-five guys out, mostly longboarders and kooks paddling for junk. They liked to surf Ponto when it was good—there were groups of pro surfers who lived across the street, seven or eight guys sharing a three-bedroom house, and they would rip it when it was on fire. Sometimes, they would see someone huge like Taylor Knox effortlessly paddling into overhead bombs, getting barrels and dominating the lineup. They knew that they shouldn't drop in on the pros, but they never worried about dropping in on the kooks and they already had reputations as fearless groms who would paddle into anything.

They rode through Oceanside and the landscape changed. Military uniform stores popped up next to surf shops and pawn shops and they saw a whore on the corner of Michigan Avenue with a purple halter top and heavy tattoos streaking up both arms. "Nice tats and tits," Cory said to Joseph.

The whore heard him. "Fuck you kids. You don't even have hair on your nuts. And you sure don't have money. Don't look at my shit unless you have the balls and the scratch to pay for my shit." She made a short run at the boys and Cory and Joseph pedaled hard to get away from her. "Get the fuck out of Oside and don't come back until you're ready for me," the whore screamed and laughed.

They rode to the gate at Camp Pendleton and a young Marine sentry waved them through. They made their way through the base with the barren, dry mountains to the east. They could see tanks doing maneuvers and a huge helicopter landed on a cliff above the ocean. They heard there were secret spots on the base that only the Marines could surf and Cory thought about surfing the base with no one out—just a clean, peaky beach break with barrels all to themselves and the occasional blasts of heavy artillery in the background.

AT DUSK THEY RODE into Trestles and walked to the beach with their boards and backpacks. It was good enough to paddle out, and they shared waves with forty of their closest friends, dropping in carelessly and getting dirty looks from balding, middle-aged men. They surfed well into the dark, squinting to see the sets coming and getting caught inside on the biggest sets, but they didn't care. They got out of the water and had to search for their backpacks and made their way north to Cottons to hide from the rangers who occasionally patrolled the beach at night. They ate beef jerky and peanuts for dinner and washed it down with a Dr Pepper. Cory got out a can of spray paint, a nice pewter gray, and he sprayed into the bag that had held their dinner. They passed out on the beach underneath the house where Richard Nixon lived. Thirty-five years ago, on summer nights just like this, Nixon used to turn the air conditioning on full blast and then light his huge fireplace to feel warm and secure, believing that the bastards were out to get him.

Cory and Joseph woke up with flecks of gray paint on their faces and they were hungry and cold and had sand in their hair. They walked to the ocean and rinsed their faces.

"You've got a spot on your ear," Joseph said.

"Thanks, Broseph. You've got something on your nose. Don't know if it's a huge boogey or paint," Cory said.

It was clean and glassy and they surfed for an hour mostly by themselves, trading waves and enjoying the rare solitude of uncrowded surf. When they got out of the water, the paint was washed away and they were ready to get back on the road. They figured that they could get to Newport, maybe beyond. They rigged up their bikes and made their way through San Clemente. It was a quiet beach town and there were only a few hills where they had to push. They rode without talking, their stomachs rumbling. At a 7-Eleven Cory bought a chocolate Yoo-hoo while Joseph stole a couple of packages of doughnuts.

They shared the Yoo-hoo on the road, passing it back and forth and stuffing tiny powdered sugar doughnuts in their mouths and they were content.

Around four o'clock, they got into Newport Beach—they were dead tired and their legs were jelly. They thought La Jolla was over the top, but it was nothing compared to Newport. There were BMWs and Bentleys and Lamborghinis everywhere, and the moms and even the grandmas had huge tits and their faces were pinned back tight like Chihuahuas ready to bite. A white Range Rover with a blonde on a cell phone pulled into their bike lane, and Cory hit the curb and went down. "Fucking bitch," Cory yelled. The woman casually put her left hand out the window, her right hand cradling the cell phone and her knees on the wheel, and flipped the boys off.

Cory had heard that 56th Street fired on a south swell and they kept on pedaling north, even though they had nothing left. When they got to 56th Street, the wind had died down and it was working. A-frame peaks were breaking up and down the beach and the locals were getting covered on every wave. Cory and Joseph could see them through the tubes, crouching in perfect position, like mosquitoes in amber. They grabbed their boards, dropped their bikes on the beach and made the short paddle to the lineup. There was no need for a wetsuit in Orange County in late summer—they just wore their camo trunks.

The local crowd gave them the stink eye, and surfers casually maneuvered to each side of them. A set rolled in and Cory and Joseph knew that they were being blocked, with locals paddling hard for every wave that was near them. Still, they were patient and quiet. And then Joseph saw a perfect peak pop up right in front of him and he whipped around in one motion and with a quick paddle he was in the wave and barreled on takeoff. He couldn't see down the line, where a kid in a custom orange and black full suit dropped in on the shoulder, coming down hard on Joseph, knocking him off his fish.

"You fucking dick," Joseph yelled as he popped up out of the water.

"Eat shit," the kid said.

"Why don't you bring it?"

"Right now."

They slogged through the knee-high water to the beach, and Joseph was the first one on the sand. The local was older and taller than Joseph, but that didn't matter. The local didn't know that Cory was paddling in right behind him, and when the local got to the beach Cory tackled him from behind. While the local was on the ground, Joseph kicked him hard in the stomach while Cory landed long rights to the back of his head.

Quickly realizing that he was outmatched, the local managed to break free and started running down the beach.

"Pussy," Joseph yelled at him. He and Cory saw the local's board in the sand and they both jumped up and down on it like wild chimpanzees, breaking the board in half and then throwing the sections as far as they could. The local stopped about fifty feet from them and watched them trash his board. "Why don't you come back and get some more?" Cory screamed. The local didn't want any more and knew that his parents would buy him a new stick when he told them the story of the kook kids from Anaheim who jumped him for no reason. He turned and kept walking down the beach.

They paddled back out well away from the pack at 56th Street and found a peak. The takeoffs were steep and they pulled into tube after tube. There were closeouts that they knew they wouldn't make but they took off on everything and occasionally bounced off the sand bottom hard. Joseph was paddling back to the lineup when he saw Cory catch a big set wave, watched him take off behind the peak and get covered with a smile on his face and hold tight to the wave and stay in the green pit for about three seconds and then kick out. They both hooted like a pack of coyotes.

It was a perfect hour of surf, the best of the trip, and then just like that the tide changed and the wind got on it and it was over. They came in, put their boards on their racks and started riding down Prospect. Riding through a stop sign, they heard the staccato whoop of a siren and looked back and there was a motorcycle cop with his lights on. They kept on riding until the cop pulled up beside them and waved for them to pull over.

"How are you boys doing today?" the cop said after he got off his motorcycle, a new, quiet BMW. He was a big man with broad shoulders and Cory smiled at his bad mustache, which had a big gap in the middle of his lips and made him look like a used car salesman. Cory didn't know that in Newport Beach, all of the cops were the same—big, broad and humorless. They lived in places like Stanton and were hired by the fine citizens of Newport to ensure that the rabble was taken care of and their homes and vintage Mercedes were protected.

"All right," Joseph said.

"You know that you guys ran through that stop sign back there," the cop said.

"I didn't really see it," Cory said.

"Well, I'm going to have to give you a ticket," the cop said.

"For what?" Cory said. "Riding through a stop sign on my bike?"

"Cyclists need to obey traffic laws, son, just like cars," the cop said.

"Fucking bullshit," Joseph whispered under his breath.

"What did you say?" the cop asked.

"Why do you have to roust us?" Joseph said. "Don't you have other stuff to do?"

"I want you to listen to me, you little shit," the cop said. "You want me to run your ass to the juvenile detention center in Orange? I know that there are some Mexicans that would love to see your blonde little ass. Are you ready to go?"

"No," Joseph said.

"Then shut the fuck up."

The cop gave each of them a ticket. "You can send in your payment or appear in court. It's your choice. Remember boys, when you are in Newport Beach, you need to obey all traffic laws," he told them and got on his BMW.

IN THE BOLSA CHICA WETLANDS there's a trail marked by a handful of palm trees that leads to a scrubby stand of coastal oak, and Cory and Joseph crawled into the tiny forest right before it got dark. They used their traffic tickets to start a small fire with deadwood they gathered and roasted four ears of corn they bought for seventy-five cents at a Mexican market in Huntington Beach, where Joseph also managed to steal a tall can of Budweiser. The beer tasted good with the corn and they wrapped up in their towels and used their wetsuits as pillows.

"So where do you want to go next?" Cory asked.

"I don't know. Where do you want to go?" Joseph said.

"Do you want to head back home, Broseph?" Cory said.

"Fuck no, brah. Nothing there," Joseph said.

"Good. Let's keep going north. We're getting waves," Cory said.

They fell asleep early and woke up at dawn and hit the road. Sunset Beach felt like Leucadia, and they splurged and bought a real breakfast at Breaker's. They walked in with sand in their hair and dirty board shorts and T-shirts and it didn't matter—that was how the majority of the customers looked at Breaker's. A waitress with long blonde hair pulled into a French braid and countless lines on her face from years of playing beach volleyball told them to sit wherever they wanted. Cory got scrambled eggs and bacon and hash browns and a bagel, and the hash browns were just right, cooked in bacon grease and butter on the long, stainless steel grill that was manned by a young Vietnamese cook who was effortless with a spatula. Joseph ordered the large stack of blueberry pancakes with a side of sausage and he covered everything in syrup and powered down a big glass of milk and burped loudly at the end of the meal. No one in the restaurant cared.

At Long Beach the Coast Highway took them inland and they saw a sign letting them know they had entered Los Angeles County and the bike lane disappeared and the surf shops and diners were replaced with signs for Ace Cash Express and Al's Bedroom Kingdom, which had been closed and abandoned for years. The street was littered with thirty-year-old white guys wearing Lakers jerseys. A lowered Impala full of *eses* cruised by and the homeboys stared hard at them and laughed.

"Hey *vatos,* where's the surf?"

Cory and Joseph kept their heads down and didn't say a word. They watched the cars parked on their side of the road closely, preparing for doors to fly open in front of them. They rode through San Pedro and saw row after row of huge containers that held bananas from Managua and DVD players from Seoul and worthless widgets from Beijing, and Cory remembered his grandfather's stories about what he called San Peeedro. Cory's grandfather told him about being a Merchant Marine during World War II, and when he got off his ship after being out to sea for months, he would end up at the bars in Peedro for days, drinking shots of Jack Daniels and fighting with navy sailors and fondling whores when he could.

When they got to Palos Verdes, the world changed again. The check-cashing and liquor stores were replaced with neat chains—Crate and Barrel and Pier 1 and the Olive Garden. Torrance, Redondo, Hermosa and Manhattan only looked slightly different and finally they found respite in Venice Beach, where they stopped on the boardwalk and a homeless Rasta with dreads and a tie-dye shirt offered to smoke a joint with them in exchange for some of the hot peanuts and jerky they were eating.

"How far is it to Hollywood by the Sea?" Cory asked the Rasta.

"Hollywood isn't far. Melrose is where you want to hang."

"Not Hollywood. Hollywood by the Sea."

"Hollywood is close to the sea. Yeah, pretty close."

"Never mind, dude."

They napped on the beach and when they got up around three their legs were sore and their shoulders hurt. Still, they were driven to go north. When they hit Malibu, they saw the coast open up before them. They could see Point Dume in the distance and the curves of the highway and the rolling hills and they knew they couldn't go any further.

"Fuck this shit," Joseph said. He was covered in sweat and the steady afternoon onshore wind was hitting his surfboard like a sail, pushing him east.

"Maybe we can hitch a ride," Cory said.

"Go for it dude. I'm beat," Joseph said.

They laid their bikes down and Cory stuck out his thumb while Joseph rested against his bike. They got lucky—around dusk a green 1970s Ford F-100 long bed pickup stopped and a Mexican boy about their age who was sitting in the corner of the bed spoke to them.

"Where are you going?" he said.

"Ventura," Cory said. "Hollywood by the Sea."

"I surf that place sometimes," the Mexican boy said. "It's hollow and fun on the right swell."

The boy looked into the cab where three men with straw cowboy hats were sitting and spoke to the driver.

"Los chicos quieren a ir a Ventura. Es posible?" he said.

"No hay un problema," the driver said. *"Vámonos."*

"Get in," the boy said.

"Thanks so much, brah," Joseph said. "We really need the ride."

The boy said his name was Alvaro and his family worked the strawberry fields of Oxnard. He said he was a bodyboarder and surfed the beach breaks of Ventura, getting up early with his father and uncle on weekends. They would drop him off on their way to the fields and pick him up at sunset. Cory and Joseph had a bag of Fritos and they shared their chips with

Alvaro and talked about glassy mornings and getting deep.

As they sat in the back of the pickup, Cory and Joseph could smell the oil and gas of the old V-8. They looked to the ocean and they could see more points in the distance and there was a small pack of surfers at County Line, quietly waiting for the inconsistent sets. It was the best they had felt all day, knowing that they wouldn't have to push up any more hills and they marveled at the miles of undeveloped coastline—no stores and no traffic—and thought this was why they went on this road trip. They fell asleep and woke up in Oxnard, where the truck had stopped in a huge apartment complex. Young mothers holding babies stood outside and talked in Spanish, laughing children rode pink and blue Big Wheels in the parking lot, and Cory and Joseph could smell beef cooking on the kettle barbecues.

"We're in Oxnard," Alvaro said. "Close to Hollywood by the Sea. Are you hungry?"

Joseph wiped some drool off the left side of his mouth with the back of his hand from his brief nap. "Absolutely," he said.

With Alvaro and his family, they ate carne asada burritos with fresh salsa and guacamole—it was as good as Lucia's, maybe better. They nodded their heads to Alvaro's father and thanked him for everything.

"Alvaro, we should probably get going," Cory said. "You saved our lives, dude. Maybe we'll see you in the water tomorrow."

They thanked Alvaro's father again and they admired his striped white cowboy shirt with the silver snap buttons—it was the same kind of shirt that surfers wore.

"Ten cuidado, chicos. Y pasan una buena noche," Alvaro's father said.

"What did he say?" Joseph asked.

"He said be careful and have a good night," Alvaro said.

Alvaro told Cory and Joseph how to get to Hollywood by the Sea and they rode off into the night down Channel Islands Boulevard. Cory and Joseph didn't know that Hollywood by the Sea was just a name for a nondescript stretch of beach that looked no different from the south side of Oceanside Jetty or 56th Street in Newport, with faceless beach houses to the east and a navy base to the south. For them, the night was warm, they could taste the bite of raw jalapeños and Cory still had the pewter gray can of spray paint in his backpack that they had saved for the end of the trip.

They were just kids as they rode on their mountain bikes, excited about the prospect of a new break. Cory thought about surfing in the morning with a pod of dolphins and the dolphins would get air, punching through the back of waves and swimming so close that Cory could touch them. It would be like a SeaWorld show, but it would be real. Fucking real.

Brother Ray

I WAS BREAKING DOWN AFTER A GIG at this dump of a bar in Oceanside when I saw this little man start walking toward me. I knew what was going to happen. You see, I have this gift—I attract the black hole of need in the universe. If someone is crazy or depressed or worried, they can spot me a mile away and they know that I'm the guy they can dump all of their grief and misery and despair on. It happens to me all the time—with friends, family and total fucking strangers.

"I really liked your guitar playing," the little guy said. "I love guitar music and you just sounded so good tonight."

"Thanks, man. I really appreciate that," I told him.

"My name is Ray," he said. "I just live around the corner. I can walk here and crawl home if I need to."

Ray was rail thin and no more than five six, with gray stubble and thick glasses. He smelled like cheap beer and cigarettes and he had some problems wiping his ass well. That's my other gift—I have an incredibly keen sense of smell, and let me tell you, there are far more bad smells in the world than good ones.

"My daughter plays guitar," Ray told me. "I bought her one when she was little. She's coming out to see me next week from Indiana. I get so lonely and I really miss her. Sure will be good to see her."

"That's nice, Ray. It's always good to see family."

"Maybe we'll come out to see you play next week. My daughter can really sing. You know, I'm gonna inherit a million dollars. When I do, maybe one night I'll come up here and give you a thousand dollar tip."

"Oh, Ray, you shouldn't do that. You need to take care of your family."

"Sure, I'll take care of my family. But I want to take care of good people, too. You know, I can tell. You're good people."

"Thanks, Ray, I appreciate that," I said. I was trying to make as little eye contact as possible to avoid the inevitable. But I knew it would come. And it did.

"I'm just so lonely. I wish my daughter would come out more often. I've been divorced three times. Never had a good wife. They all cheated on me. You know, I'm a little guy. Sometimes I thought they cheated because my dick was too small. But I'm good people. Don't you think I'm good people?" he said. He started to tear up and his Coke-bottle glasses magnified the tears.

"Sure, Ray, you're good people," I said.

He reached out and shook my hand and then he grabbed me above the wrist with his other hand. The next thing I know his head was buried right above my solar plexus and the son of a bitch was crying like a baby. This is my fucking life.

"You're my friend," Ray blubbered. "You're the salt of the earth. I really need more friends like you. What's your name?"

"My name is Will."

"You're my friend, Will."

THE NEXT SATURDAY we were setting up at the same bar and I was hoping that I wouldn't see Ray. I was in a bad mood and yelled at Hank, the saxophone player in the band.

"Can't you book us in any place better than this shit hole? You always tell me you have skills. What are your fucking skills? Can't you at least find us a place that doesn't smell like ass where we have to play in front of a bunch of old, ugly white folks?"

"Just plug this cable into the speaker and shut the fuck up," Hank said. "At least you're tall and good for something."

I looked at the front door and in walked Ray and there was a woman behind him with a guitar case in her right hand and I knew I was in trouble. Christ ... Jesus Christ. She was about five-eight, much taller than Ray, with auburn hair and green eyes that looked a lot like mine. People always tell me that my eyes look like the ocean on a sunny, crisp day. She had on a sleeveless denim shirt and her arms were taut and and a little sunburned and she walked like she was ready for anything that came her way.

Beauty is a funny thing. You look at someone like Angelina Jolie with her Hollywood parents and it all makes sense. She's got the right genes and her parents had enough money to get her overbite fixed when she was young and she just has it together. And then you look at Ray and his daughter and you think: How in the fuck can this happen? How can this stinking old man have a daughter like that?

Ray made a beeline toward me and his daughter walked beside him and he pumped my hand and grabbed me on the wrist again.

"Will, it's so good to see you," he said. He talked to me like we had been buddies for years. "This is my daughter, Valerie."

I did my best to stay cool, to not talk too fast or look at her tits, which were just about perfect. You see, I have a presence, too—maybe that's why the black hole makes its inevitable way toward me. People think that because I'm tall and lean and my teeth are straight and my eyes are clear that I have the answers.

They don't know that I don't have any goddamned answers, that I just scuffle through life like everybody else.

"Your dad is good people," I told Valerie. "Your dad was telling me last week that you can sing like a bird. How about sitting in with us for a few songs."

I broke the cardinal rule with that line. You rarely ask people to sit in with you, and you never ask people you've never heard before if you can possibly help it. I don't know how many times we've had fools beg to sit in with us while their drunken friends are telling us how good they are. They get on stage and bump into the microphone and have no concept of what it is to sing on time or in key and they don't have the sense to know how absolutely horrible they are and they keep on asking to do one more. And depending on your mood, you either tell them what a pleasure it was to play with them and you've got a show to do. Or if you're half-drunk and mean, like I am on more nights than I should be, you tell them that they're done and they need to get off the fucking stage before I ram my Telecaster up their ass.

But there I was looking at Valerie, hoping that she would sit in and praying that she could sing and that she wouldn't embarrass me in front of the band. I didn't really care if they gave me shit so long as she was passable and she felt good about my offer to get on stage.

"I'll sing a few with you," she said. She had a big voice with a little growl in it. Wilson Pickett used to talk about having a little corn bread in his voice—that's the kind of voice she had.

"Do you know 'Dark End of the Street' or 'People Get Ready' or 'Baby I Love You' or some stuff like that?" she asked. I was falling for her harder every time she opened her mouth.

"We can do those songs. You call the song and the key and we'll kick it off. I'll bring you up at the end of the first set. You can bring your guitar or I can cover the guitar parts for you."

"My dad says you can play. Let's see what you got," she said and smiled.

"Just be ready when I call you up," I said. Christ. What was a brother to do? Here I was, the guy with the answers, with the quick comebacks and glib remarks, and that was the best I could come up with.

I walked to the tiny stage and strapped on my guitar. I told Hank that we would end the set with a special guest from the audience and looked over to Valerie. He looked at me and knew that I was in over my head. I glanced at Drummer Bob and Curtis, our skinny bass player with no ass, counted off "T-Bone Shuffle" and we were off. As far as guitar players are concerned, T-Bone Walker is everything to me. He was this wildly creative, hip guy from Texas who invented electric guitar the way it should be played. He did splits on stage and played behind his back and duckwalked—all the shit that Chuck Berry and his followers would later make famous—and played in this amazingly fluid and distinctive style that no one had ever heard before. Of course, there wasn't a single person in the audience who knew who T-Bone Walker was—the best you could hope for was they might have heard his name on an Allman Brothers album, maybe when the Allmans did "Stormy Monday" at the Fillmore and Gregg mentioned who wrote the song.

I didn't really care at that point if we had any enlightened folks in the audience—I was just trying to sell the song. I glanced at three young fat girls at the bar, showing everything they had with their tight wifebeaters, smiled at the loaded blue-haired couple on the dance floor and then locked in on Valerie:

Let your hair down baby
Let's have a natural ball
Let your hair down baby
Let's have a natural ball
If you don't let your hair down baby
We can't have no fun at all

I played a long solo, digging in the back pickup to get the T-Bone sound, and walked out in the audience with my long guitar cord trailing behind me. I was breaking every rule I could. You need to wait until later in the night to walk in the crowd, but there I was showing everything *I had* on the first fucking song. At least I had something to show, I thought.

We worked our way through the first set and it was a pretty good crowd for Oceanside. Three Marines were hitting on the fat girls at the bar and they danced to "Big Legged Woman" (we did the Freddy King version) and we kept them on the floor for a couple more songs and then I decided it was time to bring Valerie up. I nodded at her and she walked to the stage like she had done this a thousand times before, lowering the mike like a pro. I got close to her and she smelled clean—she had bathed in something that had a hint of ginger in it—and asked her which key for "Dark End of the Street." She said G, which was the original key in the James Carr recording. I kicked on the tremolo and it warbled like a brown face Fender should. I moved from the G to the F-sharp minor to the E minor; that minor thing makes the whole song. It gives the song that hopeless quality, that even though they're finding love in some dark alley, you know it's not going to work out for them. Valerie let us go through the intro three times before she started singing. She had that Muscle Shoals vibe, the grit in her voice and the sense to take her time and not show too much. When you listen to the great black singers live, whether it's Ray Charles or

Aretha Franklin or Mavis Staples, you always hear them tell the band: *Take your time, fellas. Take your time.* Most white singers don't get that—Valerie absolutely got it. We locked into her vocal and I could see the whole band grinning and glancing at Valerie's ass.

After the bridge Valerie looked at Hank for a solo. Hank may not be the best cat to book the band, but he is a tremendous tenor player. He can get that smooth Lester Young sound or he can honk like Fathead Newman. He played the first twenty-four bars looking at the crowd and then the motherfucker walked over to Valerie and got on his knees, his vintage Selmer shining brightly, and hit those beautiful, squeaky high notes that were just on the edge of being in tune, with Valerie smiling and shaking her finger at him. I knew the band couldn't give me any shit for bringing her up on stage now.

We moved to "People Get Ready," a little faster than the Impressions' version, but Valerie didn't sound like Curtis Mayfield. She sounded big like Etta James and when we got to the part where it modulates a half step, I gave her the look and she was right there with me. And then it was my turn to solo, and I played the melody sparingly and pleadingly and got right next to her and she moved toward me on the bent notes. I could feel my balls tingle like when I was in high school looking at the crack of Katie Wilson's firm ass when she bent over to pick up a pencil. I was in a world of trouble and we hadn't even finished the first set.

We ended with "Baby I Love You" and the Marines and the fat chicks were back on the dance floor with the sloppy ancient drunks and the usual group of middle-aged white people with bad teeth who came to our shows. Hank was answering Valerie's "baby, baby, baby I love you" right on cue. The rhythm section was tight and funky and I had the band bring it down at the end of the song and we faded out with the tremolo ringing on the A seventh.

I walked with Valerie over to Ray's table. He was beaming and had that I-told-you-so look.

"What do you want to drink, Ray?" I asked.

"A Miller Lite for me," Ray said.

"I'll have a Guinness," Valerie said.

I got the attention of the waitress, with whom I had spent plenty of late nights listening about how hard it is to raise a kid on your own when your fucking ex doesn't give you a dime of child support and your kid has ADD and is having problems with math and they won't give you a tutor or extra help...

"Hey, Candy. A Miller Lite, two pints of Guinness and three shots of Bushmills," I told her. The pay wasn't good at the bar, but all the drinks were on the house. I figured I looked like a hero ordering beer and good booze.

Candy came back promptly and set up the three shots. I was a little concerned about Valerie drinking the shot. Most women you run into are a little reticent about shooting whiskey, certainly early in the night.

"Here's to good company and good people. Bushmills is good for your voice," I said and looked right at Valerie. "Not that you need any help with that voice of yours."

She threw down her shot with only a slight grimace and Ray and I were right with her. When I'm feeling magnanimous, I try to figure out what skills people have. Everyone should have some sort of skill, and I figured out Ray's—he could drink shots well. He looked utterly content after he drank the Bushmills, so content that I waved at Candy and ordered another round for us. Neither Ray nor Valerie minded, although I could see that Ray was ready to drink shots all night and it was clear that Valerie was in a good space now and didn't need anything else.

I played the rest of the gig with just the right edge, half drunk and relatively happy for once, and the bar felt right to me. On any night in the dumps that I play, you see two types of crowds. There's the rage-filled crowd that you can just feel is ready to explode with the slightest provocation. The kind of crowd where an old man will get in a fight with some twenty-year-old and neither one will feel bad about it afterward. That's my usual crowd, but hell, that's me most nights. And then there are those rare nights when you can feel drunken joy, when the crowd is grooving and dancing and strangers are buying drinks for each other and the night ends and everyone is hugging and making plans to go out for a nice, greasy breakfast somewhere. That was the crowd when I met Valerie. We ended the last set and they were yelling for one more and I looked over to Valerie and nodded at her to come on stage. I went right into the opening riff of "Mustang Sally," even though I've played that song so many times that I hate it. I knew the crowd wanted to sing and dance and I figured Valerie would know the words.

Valerie was right on the money and the crowd screamed the drunken refrain "ride, Sally, ride" off and on for ten minutes and we ended hard and we were done. Valerie looked up at me with a smile and I gave her a hug and her chin was in my chest and she still smelled like ginger and I hoped I wasn't too funky.

"It was really a pleasure to play with you. You can flat out sing, girl."

"This made my trip. There aren't a lot of good soul bands in fucking Indiana."

"I haven't talked to the fellas, but I'm pretty goddamned

sure that if I make you an offer to join the band, they won't complain too much. Why don't you move back? Just think. You can play in lovely Oceanside and if we get lucky we can book something in Escondido or Jamul. You can be close to the old man and I'll buy him shots every time I see him."

"You know I think about moving back sometimes. But my kids are happy at their school and we have a house. It's a small, shitty little house, but I own it and I can make the payments. I sure couldn't afford a house if I moved back and I can't handle living in an apartment again."

I didn't want to know anything else about her kids and I didn't mention anything about my wife and kids.

"Why don't we go take a drive after I break down and get something to eat?" I asked her.

"Works for me," she said. "I'll go tell my dad that I'll be home later."

WE DROVE DOWN THE 101 at three in the morning with the windows down. The fog was starting to roll in and the air was crisp.

"How about some *menudo* or a *carnitas taco?"* I asked Valerie.

"Soul music and real Mexican food. Two things you can't get in Indiana," she said.

We stopped at Lucia's and the place was packed. Late night drunks and lost skaters lined up outside the door. I saw my friend Ernestina barking out orders.

"Carne asada burrito. Rolled tacos with guacamole. California burrito."

I got to the front of the line and Ernestina looked up and shook her head.

"Buenas noches. Como estas, mi chica?"

"Asi, asi, Will. Que quieres?"

"Dos carnitas tacos y dos tacos al pastor."

"Bueno."

"Gracias, bonita. Que tengas una buena noche."

"Vete, Will."

We ate outside at a picnic table. I loaned Valerie my heavy leather jacket and she seemed content. We talked about the dives we played and there was cornbread in Valerie's laugh and the fog was getting thicker. We drove to Ponto and walked along the beach. I brought along an old Mexican blanket that I used to wrap around my amp. We walked north toward a lifeguard tower that I knew was occasionally left unlocked. I climbed the short ladder and waved Valerie up, pulling her up by her wrist. There was no lock on the latch and I opened the plastic door and it was dark inside. I put the Mexican blanket down, set up my leather jacket for our pillow and looked up at the ceiling. We didn't need to talk at this point—we knew what was going to happen.

I touched her ear and started rubbing her nipple and it was hard. I had that feeling of anticipation like when I was a teenager and Katie Wilson gave me my first blow job in my Mercury Capri. We got naked and I went down on Valerie and she had that slight smell of ginger. She moistened up quickly and gyrated slowly. I moved up her stomach, kissing her belly button and nipples and then she went down on me and it was every bit as good as that afternoon so long ago with Katie Wilson.

We fucked slowly and then hard and we could feel the lifeguard tower moving beneath us. We didn't mind the cold or the fog. A half hour after we finished I surprised myself and was ready to go again and Valerie was too and it was longer and better the second time. We dozed for a little bit and then got up and got dressed and made our way back to the car.

"Where does your dad live?"

"In one of those apartments off Pacific."

"I'll take you there."

I parked in front of Ray's apartment complex and looked at Valerie.

"So, what's next? Can I see you tomorrow?"

"No, Will, you can't see me tomorrow. I'm leaving in two days and going back to my kids. You're leaving now and going back to your wife and kids."

"How about if I come by in the afternoon and we can go out and have a cup of coffee?"

"It's not going to work, Will. I think you're a good guy. Nothing extraordinary. Just a pretty good guy and a really good guitar player. And I appreciate that you let me sit in with the band. You know how these fucking family trips are. It's not vacation, it's pure obligation. So tonight I had my vacation and now I'm ready to go home."

"How about one more night of vacation? How about if I come by tomorrow afternoon and we can go to a blues jam in Cardiff. I know the fellas there and you can front the band for a set."

"I can't do it, Will. I need to spend some time with my dad and then I'm leaving early Monday morning."

"How about if I call you in the afternoon to see if you've changed your mind? What's your cell number?"

"You don't need my cell number. And I don't need your number. Let's keep this neat and clean. I really had a good time and now I need to go."

She got out of the car with the same swagger as when I first saw her walk in the bar. She didn't look back. She walked up to the second floor and opened the door gently and she was gone.

DO YOU KNOW WHY MICK JAGGER married Bianca Pérez-Mora Macías in the 1970s? It wasn't because she was this exciting activist or her French was impeccable or she had the look of one of those Brazilian supermodels even though she was from Nicaragua. It was because Bianca was a female version of Mick. She looked liked him and carried herself just like him. Mick wanted to fuck himself.

As I plodded through the week and had that sick feeling in my gut and felt like I was going to puke all the time, I realized that Valerie was a better version of me. I was close, but she was better. A better singer. A better person to front the band. A harder body. A whole lot tougher. And that's not an easy thing for someone like me to swallow.

I was setting up at the bar in Oceanside on Saturday and I saw Ray walk in. He looked up at me and smiled, but he was a beaten man. He grabbed my wrist again and buried his head in my stomach, crying like a baby.

"I miss her, Will."

And then, weak son of a bitch that I am, I teared up and

watched one large drop fall in slow motion on Ray's greasy hair.

"I miss her, too."

Grandview

IT WAS ONE OF THOSE RARE DAYS when everything was clear to me. The alarm went off at five and I got out of bed and put on my jeans, Ugg boots and a sweatshirt. I walked out of the house and looked up at the palm tree in the front yard. It was still and I nodded my head. *No wind.* I jumped in the car and headed to the 5 and made my way south.

I reminded myself to stay calm as I got off on Genesee Avenue. *Low expectations,* I thought. *Don't believe the hype.* But clearly every surfer in San Diego had expectations. When there's no swell for weeks, surfers get horny for waves. They bark at their girlfriends or wives or kids over little things. They get up early and drive to the beach hoping for something, just a few chest-high waves, and then they see the flags at Ponto or Oceanside or Del Mar before they even get to the beach, and it's already blowing onshore. They look at the Pacific and it's gray and flat and blown out and there's a collective mutter:

fucking junk. So the army of surfers drives back home and their wives and girlfriends hear the door slam and they know it's not going to be a good day.

But today was going to be different. The surf forecasters were calling for a solid head-high northwest swell coming from a storm that started in the Aleutian Islands. I turned right on La Jolla Farms Road and looked for cars. It wasn't too bad. Maybe I could beat the crowd at least for the first thirty minutes. I parked and put on my wetsuit and grabbed my board and tried not to breathe too hard. *Tranquilo, motherfucker, tranquilo.*

There's nothing better than the walk down to Blacks early in the morning. You can smell the coastal sage and the light is warm and you can see from La Jolla Cove to Torrey Pines and you get a sense, just for a moment, of how the coast looked before the developers and real estate agents took everything over. And then I heard the rhythmic patter of feet behind me. Fucking runners, I thought. And sure enough, two twenty-something surfers, wetsuits pulled down to their waists and lean and ripped, ran by me. These are the agros, the horniest of horny surfers, and I hate to see them. They start running from the moment they leave their cars, completely focused and seemingly incapable of getting tired. Thirty seconds later, a group of three runners hauled ass past me. I looked at my chest, peppered with gray hairs, and I smiled. I heard two more runners and I thought that someone must have parked a bus full of these fuckers at the top of the hill. By the time I got to Road Peak, ten guys had passed me.

I looked up the beach to Middle and North peaks, and it was worse than I thought. There were already seventy five guys in the water. They must have been coming in from Torrey Pines Gliderport, too. There was swell—head high and clean—but on every set wave there was drama and a battle. The agros paddled furiously for position, and at least four guys took off on every wave. People dropped in on each other with impunity, and you could hear the yelling from the beach.

"Fucking kook."

"Don't fucking drop in on me again."

"Fuck you, dude."

The soothing sounds of a new swell, I thought. I watched for twenty minutes, hoping that something would change, that the crowd would thin out or it would get more consistent or a random sandbar south of Road Peak would start going off and no one would see it. But nothing changed and I knew that I wanted no part of this scene and now I faced the daunting walk back up the trail to the car. There's always a hollow feeling when you have the expectation of surf, and then you don't get what you want and you try to accept it. Runners were still coming down the trail.

"How was it?"

"Firing and nobody out," I told them.

"Have a good one."

I looked up at the faceless houses on the cliff and remembered a conversation I had with one of the architects who designed the Salk Institute. He was a bombastic man with a huge nose and terrible skin who chain smoked and drank too much Scotch and had opinions about everything. "San Diego has no architectural style," he would tell anyone who would listen. "The only enduring building in this entire fucking town is the Salk." Every now and then he was right about something.

I took my wetsuit off, got in my car and drove north. Maybe I could find some place without an insane crowd. I passed Cardiff, Pipes and Swami's—at every spot there were at least thirty or forty black bodies bobbing in the water. I ended up at Grandview. It was at least a little off the beaten path and if you walked far enough from the main peak you could get waves mostly to yourself. At this point, relative solitude was the only thing I cared about.

I walked to the lookout point on the rickety wooden stairs, hoping that I wouldn't see the morning crew there. There's a group of guys at Grandview, mostly over fifty, and they meet almost every morning to drink coffee and look at the surf. They drive minivans and reliable Japanese sedans and hold their coffee close to their bodies and talk incessantly about waves and longboards and how they really got it last week. They weren't there, and when I looked down at the water I knew why—they were already surfing with sixty of their closest friends.

I stood where my Grandview buddies usually hung out, and then a guy in his twenties walked up. He was wearing an orange 7-Eleven hat slightly cocked to the right, like Eminem, and he was smoking a joint. He was a good-looking kid—curly blond hair and thickly muscled. He came right up to me, put his elbows on the railing and started a conversation.

"Do you surf?" he asked.

I had a wetsuit on and I was looking at a surf spot early in the morning, but I had to go with this.

"Yeah, I surf."

"Are you going to surf this morning?"

"I don't know yet."

"So what do you do for a living? Are you a stockbroker or something?"

"No man, I just work for a marketing firm."

"I might do that. Or maybe something else. Maybe real

estate or banking. I'm going to Cal State San Marcos."

"That's good."

"Yeah, I don't have to study too much. I've got a photographic memory. I just look at a book the day before a test, and I can get an A or a B."

"Wow, that's impressive."

I started to look around for a hidden film crew. Maybe this was a new MTV show, and I was getting punked. The old, square guy talking to some wild young dude and everyone would be laughing at me. But I didn't see any guys with secret cameras; it was just me and my new friend.

He took another hit off the fatty.

"I've got to tell you something that happened last night. This doesn't happen to white guys too much."

"Go man. Let's hear it."

"Well last night, I fucked a black chick...on the beach. I met her at the Calypso Café, we danced a little bit, and then we came down here and got naked."

"And with your photographic memory, I bet you remembered everything."

"Every...fucking...pump."

Right then, a longboarder walked by and my friend looked at him and handed him the joint. The longboarder took a long hit and handed it back. It was clear to me that our conversation was over and I walked back to the car. I started laughing, and I thought I was going to fall down as I tried to pull my wetsuit off each foot.

I made the short drive home, opened the door and saw my wife in her work clothes. She was apprehensive, knowing that it was early and I was already back.

"Well, did you get it?"

"Yeah, I got it."

Saved

MY OLD MAN SAVED PEOPLE. Make no mistake, he wasn't a religious man. He grew up in a small town in West Texas during the Depression, and his mother played organ in the Baptist Church. He used to talk about how the preacher would occasionally come to his dump of a two-room shack on Sundays, and his mother would fry a chicken and bake a pecan pie. The preacher would look at my dad, holding a drumstick in his hand, and ask if he wanted to be saved. My old man didn't care about being saved—he just wanted the other drumstick or maybe a wing. But he and his family watched dutifully as the preacher ate the best parts of the chicken while they got a neck bone or gizzards or maybe a thigh, if they were lucky.

The old man made his way to Los Angeles in the winter of 1938. He was eighteen years old and hopped a train from Abilene with scores of other desperate men who were looking for hope and new lives in California. He used to say that

Los Angeles was a magical place back then. People still lived in downtown and there were trolleys that you could catch and go all over the city, from Exposition Park to the Crenshaw district. My dad got a job at Hollywood Park—he was a barback on the day it opened in the spring of 1938, and he remembered seeing Joan Blondell and Ronald Coleman at the track that day. Blondell wore a yellow dress that highlighted her tremendous assets and Coleman sported a gray suit and that mustache of his. My old man said he always wanted to grow a mustache like Ronald Coleman, but he never could. His beard had red and brown and black in it, even when he was a young man.

Hollywood Park was a perfect place to learn how to tend bar. You had to be fast because your customers were always edgy about the race they just lost and getting their next bet placed. The bartender at my dad's station used to bark at him all the time.

"You need to be damned sure to have my mixes and setups ready, Snake," he would tell him. "And when I tell you to jump, son, you better jump." They called my dad Snake back then because he was razor slim—six feet two inches tall and a hundred and forty-five pounds. I didn't have an ass back then, my old man explained to me, I just had a hole in my back like a snake.

After a few years, he moved from Hollywood Park to Slapsy Maxie's, a hopping nightclub on Beverly Boulevard that was owned by the boxer Maxie Rosenbloom, who was the light heavyweight champion of world in the early 1930s. The old man said that Maxie was only the figurehead for the joint, that it was really run by the mobster Mickey Cohen. He didn't care either way—he loved the place. The customers wore their finest every night, and the bands were jumping. The always elegant Duke Ellington played there, and Count Basie rocked the place with his tight band from Kansas City featuring Lester Young. A young guitar player from Texas, T-Bone Walker, brought his electric guitar to Slapsy's with the Les Hite Orchestra. When my old man watched Chuck Berry play in the 1950s, he knew where he got his moves and chops from—Chuck was all T-Bone, he would tell me.

The work was good at Slapsy's until the war broke out, and the old man joined the merchant marines. He was a cook on the ship—he never liked heights and said that it would have been impossible for him to do the climbing that was required of the regular shipmates. But he was a fine cook and a tremendous poker player so he got along fine.

When the ship made port at San Pedro, the old man always got a little worried. The merchant marines was full of ex-cons and car thiefs and burglars, and they knew who had won money in the all-night poker games during their time at sea. My dad carried a fourteen-inch French knife when he got off the ship—he sharpened a knife like no man I ever knew. You could shave with any knife my old man ever touched, whether it was a tiny Case pocketknife or a cleaver. He made sure a big guy walked off the ship with him and he would slip him a twenty when everything was clear.

When the war ended, the old man stumbled into a job as a union representative with the hotel, bar and restaurant local. He always had an affinity for workers and poor people, so the union job made sense for him. He met my mom in the union office in downtown Los Angeles. He wore sharp suits and custom-made ties back then, even if he could barely afford them, and my mom immediately noticed his swagger and baritone voice. She was a secretary and had moved to California from Kansas City with several of her siblings. She looked like a poor man's version of Lana Turner, with her tiny waist and perfect skin. They got married in Las Vegas about a year after they met and moved to a small house in Inglewood. They had my sister a few years after they were married and she was a handful for them. She was colicky and had eczema and cried all the time and the old man had no patience for babies and dumped all of the parenting on my mom. When my sister was in kindergarten she befriended a black girl in her class whose name was

Erlene. My sister invited Erlene to the house and they would play with dolls and eat hot cherry turnovers that the old man made just for them.

One of our neighbors came up to my dad one day when he was out front mowing the lawn. This was the late 1950s, and there were precious few black people living in Inglewood at that time and no black folks in our neighborhood.

"Dale, we see that Linda has been playing with a colored girl. We're a little worried about having colored people in the neighborhood."

Now my old man was not the most enlightened guy out there in terms of race relations. He was from Texas, and his mom, good Baptist that she was, had an irrational hatred of black people and dashed out of the room whenever she saw a black person on television. Sure, the old man lived for Ray Charles and Muddy Waters and Count Basie, but he talked about coons and niggers on a regular basis when he was ranting about some dishwasher or cook who didn't want to join the union. No one, however, was going to tell him who his daughter could have over to his house.

"This is my property that you're on," the old man told our neighbor, Ad Swensen, who was a nice fellow from Des Moines. "And I'll have whoever in the hell I want on my property. So I advise that you get the hell away from my house, and I don't ever want to hear any more talk from you about my baby girl's friends."

Three years later I was born and we moved from Inglewood to Orange County. My parents sold their house to a hard-working black family with two kids and the old man must have been smiling as he drove the moving truck to Anaheim.

IN THE EARLY 1960s, there was a reason they called it Orange County. My friends' parents, who moved to California from Wisconsin or New Jersey, used to tell us the perennial stories about how they walked to school three miles in the snow. We laughed at them. We walked to school through orange groves and it never snowed in Southern California. Not unless your parents drove you to Apple Valley or Big Bear in the winter.

We lived in East Anaheim. My parents fought about where they wanted to live, and the old man threatened to divorce my mom if she didn't agree to live in the house that he picked. She capitulated, and we ended up on Howard Circle a few blocks away from the Santa Ana River, which was dry most of the year and only came alive during the occasional torrential rain in the winter.

My old man never made a lot of money in the union, and our

neighborhood wasn't the best. You could easily go from your house to your friend's down the street and know exactly where every room was. I didn't really care about the houses back then—the people made the place. There were the Thibodeauxs at the end of the street, a white trash family from New Orleans. The parents, Pearl and Ed, were hopeless alcoholics, and they smelled like stale beer all the time and had raucous parties in their backyard. Invariably, they would both get drunk and Ed would throw Pearl in the pool and she would start crying and their son, Bobby, who was my friend, would start crying and my old man would calm Ed and Pearl down and invite Bobby to stay with us for the rest of the night. There were the Goldschmidts across the street, another alcoholic family with three wild teenage girls. Old man Goldschmidt was drunk most of the time and he tried, loaded or sober, to reign those girls in. It was hopeless. I remember him yelling at his girl Lori to get her ass back in the house, and she proceeded to run through their yard and gracefully jump over their three-foot fence, doing her best imitation of Rod Milburn in his prime. At the apex of her jump, she casually looked back at her dad and said, "Fuck you." I saw that move many times until Lori moved out of the house at seventeen and shacked up with some motocross rider from Costa Mesa.

My dad thrived in this neighborhood. He would make huge

pots of pinto beans and barbecue ribs and whole chickens for the neighbors. They never understood why everything tasted so good—they didn't understand what my dad knew—barbecue has to involve smoke and real wood. Every now and then the old man would find calf fries at the local Stater Brothers and he would bread them and fry them up and tell everyone that they were veal cutlets. The neighbors would tell the old man those were the best cutlets they had ever eaten and he would laugh and say that they weren't really veal cutlets, they had just eaten calf balls. The neighbors would scream, "How could you make me eat calf balls?" Then they'd pause and tell the old man, almost furtively, "But they were sure good, Dale."

Word got around in the neighborhood that the old man was the go-to guy for problems. Widows and insurance salesmen would come to him for help with their plumbing or sprinklers or for some advice on cooking. When my friend David Cantelmo's mom, who was divorced, needed help with her garage door, she asked me if my dad could come over. David's grandmother, who was from Milan, lived with the family and she spoke no English. She was in her seventies and less than five foot tall with a big widow's hump and David and his mom treated her like a dog. David called her the dirt woman because she grew tomatoes and zucchini and peppers along the side of their house and stayed in the garden all the time to get away from her daughter and grandson. I told the old man that David's mom needed some help with the garage door, and he dragged me along with him to fix it.

"Hello, Mrs. Cantelmo, what's wrong with your garage?"

"It just won't open or close, Dale," Mrs. Cantelmo told him.

She looked like a vampire—she had plucked her eyebrows and painted new ones on with a brown pencil, like the Mexican women in downtown Anaheim. She wore polyester leopard-skin prints and her hair was big and hair-sprayed hard in place like Ronald Reagan's.

We walked into the garage and the old man figured out the problem.

"Well, Mrs. Cantelmo, you need a new spring."

"That's fine, Dale. I'll pay you back if you wouldn't mind picking it up for me."

We drove to the local Ace Hardware where the old man knew everyone in the store and bought the spring. Garage door springs have a tremendous amount of tension, and it takes a pretty strong man to install them. I generally dreaded doing any job with my dad because I knew he was going to scream and cuss a lot.

"Now goddammit son, when I start pulling on this spring I want you to attach it to the garage," he warned me.

He grunted and heaved and the spring moved a little bit.

"Goddammit, boy, attach the sonbitch to the door now."

"I'm trying to."

"Just do it. I can't hold this sonbitch all goddamned day."

We got the job done and Mrs. Cantelmo thanked us and the grandmother gave us some tomatoes. My old man liked the grandmother—he used to smell the *osso buco* she made and he knew she could cook. When we got in our black Ford station wagon with the fake wood panels on the sides, he told me I should always be nice to the grandmother and I should never call her the dirt woman even if she didn't understand English.

THE CANTELMOS WERE A SMALL PROJECT for the old man. The real project was the Wenners. They lived three houses down from us and they were a mess. The parents, Stan and Alice, were both deaf and they had four boys: Cole, Gary, Jeffrey and Sam. Three of the boys could hear; Jeffrey was born deaf. Cole and Gary were teenagers and they were my heroes. They were hoodlums—small-time pot dealers and bike thieves who would occasionally do a bigger project like breaking into a garage to steal tools. Sam was the youngest, but he was clearly on the path of his older brothers. I remember when he was three years old and he was standing in our cul-de-sac watching some kids play down the block. He had a deep voice even when he was a little boy.

"Hey," he yelled down the street. "What are you doing down there?"

The kids didn't respond to him.

"Hey," he said. "What are you fuckers doing down there?"

Jeffrey, who was three years older than Sam, was the only decent kid in the family. He was attentive to the world around him and he constantly tried to learn new things. His brothers tortured him, signing to him that he was stupid and excluding him from the world of the hearing whenever they could.

The Wenners regularly called on my old man to help them with tasks that hearing people took for granted. Stan was not completely deaf and wore hearing aids, but he had trouble making phone calls.

"Dale, can you make a phone call for me? I'm trying to find a cheap bike for Jeffrey."

"Sure, Stan, I know a guy at the Schwinn dealer on Broadway. Maybe we can get a deal for you."

Alice was completely deaf and used a notepad to communicate with hearing people. She would ask my mom to take care of the kids when she went to the store because she knew her boys would steal something and she would have to backhand them when they got back to the car. Still, the Wenner boys took advantage of their parents' deafness at every opportunity. They were fluent signers and they knew their parents could read lips well. They carried on emphatic conversations with their parents in sign language, but you could tell when something didn't go their way. The boys would pull their T-shirts over their mouths so their parents couldn't read their lips and scream at them: "You're full of shit, old man. I'm not going to put up with your bullshit."

That strategy endured for years until Stan, who usually kept his hearing aid off when he was at home, randomly decided to turn it on one day. He and Gary were having their usual heated conversation about curfews or school work in the front yard and Gary went to the T-shirt.

"Fuck you, you mean bastard. I'm not going to listen to your shit," Gary said.

Gary had no idea that Stan heard him and was amazed when Stan hit him with a hard right on his left ear. Gary immediately started crying and yelling.

"What did you do that for?"

Stan slowly and deliberately signed and talked to him at the same time: "You will never talk to me that way again, you little shit."

Gary ran to his room and didn't come out for the rest of

the day. Every time the Wenner boys went to the T-shirt, Stan would slap them hard on the side of their head—it didn't matter if his hearing aid was on or off. The boys eventually learned not to go to their T-shirts.

My old man had a special fondness for Jeffrey, who was the odd kid out in the neighborhood, and he would always bring Jeffrey candy from the grocery store. The old man didn't sign, but when Jeffrey signed *thank you* by putting his two fingers to his lips, the old man would sign back *you're welcome* by touching his thick fingers to his forehead and his wrist to his chest.

I REMEMBER A HOT AUGUST DAY. The old man got a call from Jim Catey, the manager of the local Alpha Beta. "You need to get down here quick, Dale," Jim said. "We have a big problem with that deaf Wenner kid."

My dad hollered at me to get moving and we jumped in the Ford wagon. The Alpha Beta was across Lincoln Avenue behind our house and the Wenners used to jump our fence to go there to steal snacks or a bottle of Boone's Farm Strawberry Hill. We made it to Alpha Beta in a few minutes and the air-conditioning felt good in the grocery store—I could have stayed there all afternoon. Jim Catey saw the old man and grabbed him by the arm. "You need to get that goddamned kid out of my store,

Dale," he said.

Catey walked with us to the candy and produce aisle. You could buy candy in bulk at Alpha Beta—the sugary orange slices or malted milk balls were right next to the apples and bananas. There was Jeffrey, with a can of gasoline in one hand and candy in the other, walking casually down the aisle. The can was obviously full and gasoline would occasionally drip out and you could smell it throughout the store. My old man walked past Jeffrey and got in front of him; Jeffrey looked up and smiled. The old man reached out his hand and gently took the gasoline can from Jeffrey and then grabbed his hand and started walking toward the door. Catey followed anxiously behind us.

"We were trying to get him to leave, but he didn't listen to us. He just kept going down the aisles with the gas can, dripping everywhere," Catey said.

"I'll pay you for the candy, Jim," my dad said.

"Don't worry about it, Dale. Just get him out of here."

Jeffrey jumped in the wagon and sat in the front seat in between the old man and me and we drove to the local gas station. The can had a Mobil logo on it, and the old man picked it up and walked up to Ray Miller, who owned the station. Miller had a big scar on his right cheek that I always thought he got from a knife fight. He was a mean son of a bitch and I hated being around him. But he was from Oklahoma and he and the old man liked to talk about barbecue and deer hunting.

"Ray, I believe this can walked away from your station for a while. Here you go."

"Thanks, Dale. I appreciate you finding it for me."

My dad got back in the car and he had an orange slice in his shirt pocket. He handed it to Jeffrey, who signed *thank you* and put his head on the old man's shoulder as we drove home.

Notes from a Federale

MY PARTNER RODRIGO AND I have conversations with twenty to thirty Americans on a good day. We patrol a small area—from *Avenida Independencia* north to *Avenida Paseo Tijuana.* We play a little game to keep our days interesting—sometimes I am the captain and sometimes it is Rodrigo.

The other day late in the morning we saw a white Toyota Sequoia with an attractive blonde woman and an old man. They looked like they were in a hurry—the Americans always seem to be in a hurry. They were close to the border and perhaps they thought soon they would go back to their jobs and their families.

The woman and the old man passed us at our usual place on *Avenida Independencia* and Rodrigo waved them down, but they did not stop. Rodrigo likes the chase and he put on his lights and pulled them over at the place where we stop all the Americans. It is a barricaded street where we can talk quietly away from the traffic.

Rodrigo walked to the driver side of the Toyota and the blonde woman, who had blue eyes and very large breasts, rolled down the window. She was wearing an expensive navy blue suit and looked like she was going to work. We don't usually see women like this. More often than not, we run into surfers or fishermen traveling for the day to get away from the crowds in San Diego or businessmen who come down for prostitutes before work.

"Is there a problem?" the woman asked. The Americans always ask this question and, of course, there is always a problem. Otherwise, we would not spend our time pulling them over.

Rodrigo speaks some English, but he started the conversation in Spanish to make the Americans nervous.

"Estabas manejado muy rápido. Esta zona es treinta kilometros. Estabas manejado cincuenta y cinco kilometros."

"I don't understand Spanish. *No habla español,*" the woman said.

"You were driving too fast," Rodrigo said. "At least twenty-five kilometers per hour too fast. You wait here. I will call my captain."

Rodrigo called me on the radio and it gave me pleasure to be the captain that morning. I rode up on my motorcycle and had a brief conversation with Rodrigo. We looked serious and occasionally glanced at the driver and I shook my head. I walked slowly up to the driver and she had the look in her eyes, the look of fear of the unknown. I see it all the time.

"How are you today?" I asked her. My English is perfect. I went to school in Solana Beach when my parents lived across the border. I started school in the first grade and by the time I was in third grade I could translate for my parents. They would take me with them to make big purchases—to buy a refrigerator or a television or a VCR. I watched a lot of television at home—reruns of *Seinfeld* and *Law and Order* and, of course, the commercials for Captain Crunch and the new Ford Mustang and joining the Army. People do not realize how useful television can be in learning a new language.

I went to elementary school and I was a very good student—we lived in Eden Gardens where most of the Mexicans in Solana Beach lived, right down the street from Tony's *Jacal* and Fidel's barbershop, where Fidel sold tamales before he started his own restaurant.

In elementary school, we would sometimes take beatings from the Anglos when they caught us alone in the bathroom or walking home from school. They would call us beaners and chase us right to the edge of Eden Gardens, but they were smart enough never to come into our neighborhood. Of course, we would return the favor when we found the Anglos without their reinforcements on the playground. Still, we got along more often than not and played together on Little League baseball and Pop Warner football teams and ate together at the taco shops that Mexicans eventually opened outside of Eden Gardens.

My family went to Tijuana every weekend to see brothers and sisters and cousins. We would buy things in Tijuana that were hard to get in Solana Beach—the sweet Mexican Coca-Colas with cane sugar and the tamales made with all the parts from a pig's head. When I graduated from high school, I returned to Tijuana and joined the Federal Police of Mexico. The fact that I was bilingual helped me get my first position and I have been with the force for ten years now. There is something about living in your own country with your own people that is much more satisfying than living abroad. I like my job most days, and I thought this would be one of those days.

"My partner tells me that you were speeding. You must be more careful when you are driving here."

"I didn't realize that I was speeding, sir," the blonde woman told me.

The Americans are, more often than not, formal and respectful when we pull them over. At least the Americans with money who know they have much to lose if they are not respectful.

"So here is the deal. This is a simple thing and it does not need to be difficult. You can be across the border and back home in thirty minutes. There is no reason to be nervous. You were speeding and the fine for this is one thousand five hundred pesos—one hundred fifty dollars."

"Officer, we don't have one hundred fifty dollars. We don't carry that much money," the woman said.

"Then perhaps we need to take you to the station downtown to discuss this."

"Then let's go to the goddamned station. My daughter is a good driver. She didn't do anything wrong," the old man said. He did not look well—he was pale and there were tiny beads of sweat above his lip.

"I am certain that your daughter is a perfect driver, sir. But my partner tells me that she was speeding, and my partner is a person with integrity. I must believe him."

"I don't believe your goddamned partner. I believe my daughter, and it's time for us to go home and leave this godforsaken country."

"Dad, please be quiet and let me talk," the woman said. She looked directly into her father's eyes and she was begging him to behave. I know this look—all too often I must go to the bars late at night to get my father when he is drunk, and I have to look into his eyes this way.

"I'm sorry. My father is not feeling well. We come here to get him medication to deal with his pain. He has problems with his back. His cancer has moved there. The doctors won't give us enough medication, so that's why we come here. I'm sure you understand. You must have a father."

"I do understand. I will do you a favor this time. You can pay a fine of one hundred dollars."

"That's highway fucking robbery. You aren't doing us any favors and my daughter wasn't speeding and we don't have a hundred dollars to give to you."

"Dad, for Christ sake, can you *please* be quiet?"

"Cállate, pinche viejo." Now Rodrigo was part of the conversation.

"Sir, you cannot speak to me and my partner like that."

"I can talk any way I goddamn please to you. I want to talk to your superior. There's not anything right about this. We weren't doing anything wrong and I feel like hell and I want to go home."

The old man coughed up a large piece of phlegm and spit on Rodrigo's motorcycle. I know that he didn't mean to get so close to the motorcycle, but then it was too late. Rodrigo pulled the passenger door open and grabbed the old man by the back of his neck. The old man had no strength and went limp—Rodrigo lost his grip and the old man crumbled on the street and hit his head hard and started to bleed from a cut on the top of his head.

"What is fucking happening?" the woman screamed. She was out of the car and crying and her father was bleeding and she held his head in her arms as he bled on her suit. "Why did you have to do this?"

It was hard to tell if she was talking to Rodrigo or her father or me. Her father was on the street and not talking—he looked defeated now. Any cut on the head bleeds heavily. Strings of the old man's gray hair hung down in his eyes and I could tell he would need stitches to close the wound on his head.

"Pinche viejo. Entonces, no puedes decir nada."

"Tranquilo, Rodrigo. Tranquilo."

The woman looked at me with hatred in her eyes now. She laid her father's head gently on the pavement and opened the purse that was over her shoulder. She went quickly through her wallet. "We only have ninety six dollars," she told me and started to hand me the money.

"Fold the bills up in your hand and pass me the money slowly."

"Can you please help me get my dad back in the car?"

I lifted her father up underneath the pits of his arms and he smelled like death. He weighed nothing, really, and he was probably a good man, but he should not have talked to my partner and me like that. I like the Americans—truly I do. They provide for me and my family and my country. But they need to understand that there are rules here—the rules are not simple. Little of the money that Rodrigo and I collect each day goes to us. Much of it will go up the chain to watch commanders and assistant police chiefs and superintendents. And then there are the cartels—if we do not pay them, we may come home one day and find that our children are missing or our wives have been raped. In Michoacan the *narcotraficantes* walk the streets and take any woman they want, and there is very little any man can do.

I went to my motorcycle and opened up the saddlebag to get out my first-aid kit. I handed the woman a bandage and some gauze. "This will help until you get your father to a doctor."

"I don't need any Band-aids from you. I just want to go home," the woman told me. She was trying to hold back her tears now.

"Then I want you to follow my partner and he will get you back on the road to the border crossing. Remember to be more careful when you are driving in Mexico."

When Rodrigo met me back at our regular place, he was smiling.

"I have been thinking that you need to change your speech to the Americans," Rodrigo said. "You need to tell them the truth for once. You need to tell them that you are here to fuck them in the ass and take their money. But it will not hurt too much because your dick is not that big and they can always get more money."

Perhaps Rodrigo is right.

Perhaps this is about painless fucking. But the Americans do not understand this. They want to fight the inevitable. And over nothing of consequence—fifty dollars or one-hundred dollars. I did not like to see that old man bleeding. He reminded me too much of my father—stubborn and mean. He could not face that his life was over and he should try to live without conflict and needless drama, without holding on to meaningless principles. Maybe my father lived in America too long. I am glad that I left that place.

Nada Es Nada

THERE WAS NOTHING I HATED MORE than to see my old man cry. He was a big man, about six two and he weighed every bit of two-sixty. When he cried his whole body shook and he made a high-pitched noise that just didn't fit his frame.

Around three in the morning I came into the house loaded on Crown Royal and Quaaludes and the old man was sitting at the dinner table blubbering like a baby.

"What's wrong, Dad?"

"Something bad happened tonight, son. Something real bad."

He lifted his head up and pulled it together. My old man had a huge head. He used to joke that he was the only man he knew with a size eight hat. Clear mucous ran down both nostrils and he wiped it off with the back of his hand. He had big, thick hands. It always amazed me that he used those hands to bake elegant pecan pies and he would use the leftover dough to make me turnovers with homemade blackberry jam.

"Fred Lasley called me while I was watching the Bob Newhart Show and said he needed me. He was a wreck. He said the cops just called him and Alan was in a bad accident and he needed to come down to the hospital right now."

"Did he wreck his motorcycle again?"

"Shut up and let me tell the goddamned story. Fred said that he couldn't drive. I picked him up and we went to the emergency room at that hospital in Irvine. The one where your sister used to work. Fred was shaking and crying and he didn't say much. He said the cops didn't give him any details.

"We parked at the hospital and I got out of the car and Fred just sat there. I told him we needed to get moving. He said that he couldn't move. He said he couldn't take seeing his boy with more broken bones. He said maybe it was going to be worse this time. I opened his door and grabbed him by his shoulder and told him we needed to go see Alan.

"We walked into the emergency room and I talked to this cold bitch at the front desk. A goddamned Filipino. I said we were here to see Alan Lasley, that the police had called us. She looked down at a sheet of paper and told us to sit down and wait. Nothing more than that. Just sit down and wait.

"We waited twenty minutes. Fred didn't say anything. He

just had his head buried in his hands. Then I saw this cop talk to the woman at the front desk and she pointed to us. The cop came over to us. He was a big guy with broad shoulders and a military haircut, one of those prick Anaheim cops. He asked me if I was Mr. Lasley and I told him no, this is Fred Lasley. Fred looked up at him and the cop said that he had some bad news. He said that Alan was killed in a motorcycle accident."

"Oh shit, Dad, don't tell me that."

"Just wait. Just fucking wait for me to finish the story, son. Fred rolled off his chair and got in a ball and started to howl. The cop looked at me like I was supposed to do something. I patted Fred on the back. I told him that everything was going to be all right, that he had to be strong and he had two other kids and a wife and he was going to make it. I knew it was all a fucking lie. How could he make it? How could he lose his boy and make it?

"The prick cop said that Fred needed to identify the body. I grabbed Fred underneath his armpits and lifted him up. We walked down a hallway and there were sick Mexicans lined up in hospital beds waiting to be seen by doctors. The cop opened the door to a room at the end of the hallway and there was a hospital bed covered by a sheet. You could see the shape of a body underneath it, and Fred went down on his knees again.

He said he couldn't do it. The cop said he needed to get up and identify his son. He didn't give a fuck about Fred or his son. He didn't give a fuck about anybody's son. I pulled Fred up one more time and we walked over to the sheet together. The cop lifted the sheet and we looked at the face and then Fred really lost it. It wasn't Alan. It was that Dickinson boy, Bobby Dickinson.

"Fred called the cop a cocksucker. He said that wasn't his boy and he asked the cop how could he have put him through all of this shit for nothing. The cop asked him if he was sure. I said hell yes, we were sure. Alan had black hair and this boy had long blond hair. We knew this boy—he was Alan's friend. The cop lost that cocksure look. He told us they found the boy next to a motorcycle that was registered to Fred Lasley. The boy didn't have any ID, the cop said, but we had to believe that it was Alan. There was a sticker on the back with Alan's name on it and a number. It must have been from one of those motocross races that Alan rode in.

"We told the fucking cop that he needed to contact Bobby Dickinson's folks. They lived on Virginia Avenue. He said he was sorry, but he didn't mean it.

"I drove Fred home and when he got out of the car he started running to his front door. I followed him in and I could hear him screaming in Alan's room. I walked in—I figured I was part of this whole thing and I deserved to hear the story. Alan was lying in bed drunk.

"Fred was screaming. Where have you been, you little son of a bitch? Alan said that he and Bobby were partying up in Anaheim Hills, that they rode up there together on Alan's motorcycle. He said some girls were with them and one of the girls offered to give him a ride to a party in Newport Beach. He thought Bobby would be okay. He left him the keys to the motorcycle. Fred told Alan that Bobby was dead, but the cops thought it was him. He grabbed Alan hard by both shoulders and looked into his drunken eyes and told him never to do anything like that again."

We sat at the table for another half hour and my old man didn't say anything. I was so high on the Crown and Quaaludes combo that I passed out. My dad shook me.

"Get your ass to bed, son."

I walked down the narrow hallway, trying not to bounce off the walls and wake up my mom, and fell in bed.

"Get your clothes off, boy. You can't sleep in your clothes."

My dad pulled off my shoes and I got my pants off and got under the covers. I could barely fit in the twin bed that my parents bought me when I was eleven. I was a good three inches taller than the old man and all I wanted was to get the fuck out of that house and that crazy neighborhood and start college.

"Why were you crying, Dad? You know Alan. He's my friend. But we don't know Bobby's family. And he was always an asshole to me."

"You don't understand anything, do you boy?" my old man said. "You don't understand a goddamned thing."

Baja Malibu

I WANT YOU TO LOOK AT YOUR NEIGHBOR. The cat with the wraparound Oakleys and the Old Guys Rule hat pushing his Honda lawn mower on a Sunday afternoon. He's the guy that your kids always say is "so nice." He looks like he's all right with the yard gig, but you know what he's thinking. He's fucking tired of hearing shit from his prick of a boss in the mortgage business. Another goddamned USC grad driving a 740 bimmer and shuffling meaningless pieces of paper so he can live in the smallest house in Rancho Santa Fe. As your neighbor plods behind the Honda with the slightest hint of a smile, he's thinking about taking a baseball bat to his next meeting and kneecapping his boss. He's thinking about solid contact and high screams and then dropping the bat and calmly walking out of the office.

Thoreau said we all lead lives of quiet desperation. I remember when I was in graduate school and I got in an argument with a guy from Boston named Stan Holliman about this desperation idea. We were in a seminar and Stan wanted to know how Thoreau really knew the woodcutter was desperate. He might have been just fine carrying his axe around and cutting trees, Stan argued. I declared to the class that while I respected my friend from Boston, I thought he was full of shit on this one. My classmates never liked it when I cussed, but I didn't give a fuck and always liked to create a little tension in what was otherwise a deadly boring seminar. Thoreau was right on the money on this, I said. The woodcutter didn't want to carry that axe every day. He wanted to do what Thoreau did—he wanted to put the axe down one day and just hang out in the woods and scratch his balls and fish and think about women and have a drink with his buddies. But he knew that he couldn't do that. He knew that he had to keep on cutting down trees in some forest in the middle of nowhere and he was alone and he was tired of it and he was plenty desperate. The seminar ended and we all went to the Green Leaf and I ordered a couple of pitchers and everything was good. I ordered a shot of Bushmills for Holliman and one for me; we clinked our shot glasses to cutting down trees.

Jesus, that was a long time ago. I'm driving to the San Ysidro border now, and I don't know what the fuck I'm going to do when I get there. I'm thinking about Henry Miller and I riff on one of his lines. *This then is a song. I am singing.* Not quite. *This is a song. I am screaming.*

I'M A MUSICIAN when I'm not working my day job doing public relations for a pharmaceutical company. Make no mistake—playing in front of a bunch of drunks in Ocean Beach is much more meaningful than talking with some crazy research scientist about his latest work on betamyloid and how it might have some role in Alzheimer's disease. The problem with this whole biomedical research complex is that there are a thousand scientists in places like La Jolla and Singapore and Munich all doing the same work and coming to the same inconsequential conclusions. They're holed up in cold, identical labs, taking money from big pharma or the National Institutes of Health so they can conclude, at the end of their illustrious thirty-year careers, that this gene or that one may or may not have relevance to our understanding of cancer. Of course, I never write this in the press releases I send out to reporters hungry for a news hook on the latest breakthrough for the disease of the day. I make the pitch and the reporters buy it occasionally and write an eight-inch story that's buried in the front section. They're happy their editors are happy and some woman in Des

Moines has hope that they're really going to find a cure for her husband's colon cancer.

And then I go home and hang out with the family and cook dinner. On Tuesdays, the band comes over for rehearsal. Most nights I don't know if I'm the guitar player, the band leader or the fucking staff psychologist. My horn player's wife let him know after twenty years of marriage that she's been banging his best friend the whole time they've been married, and he's been a mess ever since. My drummer is going through a divorce, and I keep on telling him it's a good thing because I always thought his wife was a bitch. Sometimes he agrees with me, and sometimes he doesn't want to hear it. Ruth, our crazy diva singer, has some ex-boyfriend stalking her who just got out of jail, and I have to follow her home after gigs, let her into her apartment and make sure the coast is clear. Our bass player, Curtis, is the only person who's in a decent space—he's a good-looking young kid always scoping the crowd and goes home most nights with a new pretty young thing.

My kids love to see the band. My daughter Lilly, who's eight, gives Ruth a big hug and they cuddle on the couch and talk about clothes or nail polish before we start to play. My twelve-year-old son Walker grabs his Stratocaster and he sits in for a couple of songs and blows a serious solo on "Cissy Strut" and we all smile. After an hour, the kids begrudgingly go up to their rooms and then we work through a new Aretha or Etta or Staples song, drink a few beers and we're ready for our next job.

Despite the drama, there's something magical about this band. A little after one in the morning, when we're in some funk bar in Pacific Beach and I turn on the tremolo and play the opening riff to "Chain of Fools" and the band locks into a groove and Ruth works the crowd of golden, drunk college students grinding on the dance floor and we bring it down to a whisper and then end hard and on time, when that happens I forget all of the bullshit and for the rest of the night everything is right with the world.

But here's the funny thing. This music thing, one of the few things that give me joy, has got me in the bind I'm in. That piece of shit guitar store in Escondido—that was my undoing. I never liked Escondido. Even my wife Carol, who's one of the most likable and affable souls anywhere, says that her skin crawls whenever she goes to Escondido. That place creeps me out, she would tell me. Maybe it was the whores, brazenly walking in front of some 1970s office buildings in the middle of the day. Maybe it was the funky downtown, where businesses shut down every six months. I should have listened to Carol, but I'm a selfish bastard.

When you're a guitar player in a working band, you're constantly on the prowl for more stuff. You're looking for some bitchen little Supro amp or a beaten up Harmony arch-top with those cool De Armond pickups. And Lost Guitars in Escondido had what I was looking for—Silvertones and Airlines, Danelectros and Alamos. The gear was right in Lost Guitars, but the owner wasn't right. His name was Larry Olsen and he desperately wanted to be a California hipster. He wore thrift shop Hawaiian shirts—bright oranges and blues and teals—that barely covered his huge white gut. He had a gray blues patch that he trimmed short and a leather necklace with some stone shaped like a prehistoric shark tooth. He just tried too hard, and you knew even before he opened his mouth and said *Howyadoin* that he was from Newark or Bayonne. He was the kind of guy who would tell you the great thing about California was you could be in the mountains in the morning and the beach in the afternoon. Like that was some huge discovery that only he and a handful of others knew about. You wanted to look at him and say I grew up here, you fucking idiot, I kind of have that one figured out.

Still, I tried to be civil with Larry and occasionally traded with him. He told me he was running a special—he wanted used gear on consignment and would only take fifteen percent.

I had a 1960s Gibson Falcon amp that I wasn't using, a solid little amp that was like a poor man's Deluxe Reverb, and I brought it in.

"Whaddaya want for it?" Larry asked.

"I need to get three hundred fifty dollars out of it."

"I'll let you know when I sell it."

"Works for me."

There was not a lot of love between Larry and me; our relationship was strictly about commerce. He occasionally had stuff I wanted and I paid him a decent price for it, and now I had something that would help him in a small way. I left the shop and figured I'd hear from Larry in a month or two.

About six weeks later I called the shop and Larry's kid answered the phone. He worked there on the weekends—not a bright kid, and like pretty much every teenager I knew he was largely incapable of engaging in conversation.

"Hey, did you sell that Gibson Falcon?"

"Lemme look."

A few minutes later he came back on the phone.

"Don't see a Gibson anywhere."

"This is Will. Have your old man call me about the Gibson when he gets in."

"All right."

A few more weeks passed, and this deal started to eat at me. I knew that Larry had sold the amp, and I wanted my money. I called him on a Thursday afternoon and he answered the phone.

"Hey Larry, this is Will. Did you move the Falcon?"

"Yeah, Will. Sold it a week ago. I'll sendya a check tomorrow."

He was friendly in a New Jersey sort of way and pretty matter of fact. I felt better about everything and thought the deal was done.

On Monday, I didn't have my check and I called him back.

"Hey, Larry. Where's my fucking check?"

"Who the fuck do ya think you're talking to. I toldja I'd send ya the check and I will."

"Let me explain this to you in simple terms, you fucking moron. You sold my amp and now I want my money. You have stolen my fucking property. You need to pay me today or I'm going to come down there and kick the living shit out of you."

"Fuck you, Will."

And he hangs up on me.

I OFTEN WONDERED WHY in sunny, laid-back Southern California there were times when violence spreads like a wildfire in the Santa Monica mountains. It usually starts in the summer, when some real estate broker from Diamond Bar gets cut off on the 57 freeway by some lawyer in an Acura. They start jawing at each other, sticking their heads out the window and flipping each other off and they pull over to the side of the freeway and the real estate guy beats the shit out of the lawyer with a tire iron. The next day, there's a shooting on the Harbor Freeway when a homeboy driving his 1966 Impala gives a Crip the wrong look and takes a 9mm slug in the chest.

And then you have a trend story in the *Los Angeles Times* on road rage and people think they need to protect themselves and start carrying .22 Rugers or .380 Berettas in their glove boxes and the next thing you know housewives and insurance executives and gang bangers are shooting at each other from the safety of their air-conditioned cars every other day. A month later six people are dead, three others wounded and then the madness stops for no apparent reason.

You think it's just the blare of a horn or the staccato scream of "asshole" that sets people off, but it's more than that. It's a lifetime of rage and slights and eating shit for no reason. At least that's my take on it. Larry didn't know that it just wasn't the right time in my life for him to steal my money and tell me to fuck off.

You see, while I was waiting for Larry to pay me, Lilly started having a problem walking. Her left leg started kicking out uncontrollably and randomly, and then she couldn't use her left hand. Carol and I took her to a pediatric neurologist, a young guy with long hair tied neatly in a ponytail. He went through the basic neuro exam and he got a scared look in his eyes and told us that Lilly needed an MRI immediately, and she and Carol started crying. I told them to go outside, trying to be as calm as I could, and that I would talk with the doc.

"Why do you think she needs an MRI?" I asked him.

"She is displaying a motion called a chorea, and it's deeply concerning to me," he said.

"Chorea, as in Huntington's chorea?"

"Yes that could be one option."

"That's a fatal disease, and I've never heard of it in children."

"I don't mean to scare you, Mr. Bartlett, but there are several serious diseases your daughter could have. Some of them could be life-threatening."

"So let me get this right. You do a neuro test, you see some symptoms and now you're telling me my daughter could have a fatal, degenerative disease."

"It's one possibility, Mr. Bartlett. There are many serious genetic diseases that present with these symptoms. Huntington's disease, pediatric multiple sclerosis, dystonia, and some even more obscure that would require a whole battery of tests to identify."

"Wait a second. This is bullshit. You can't do a simple exam and tell me immediately that my daughter might die. You need data. This is totally fucking irresponsible."

"That's why I want the MRI."

"I'm fine with the MRI, but here's what I want you to do. I'm going to bring my daughter and wife back in this room, and you're going to tell them that this is just a test. It's not anything to worry about. It's just a precaution. And you're not going to have a scared look on your face when you talk to them."

"I can do that, Mr. Bartlett."

I got Lilly and Carol and explained to them that everything was going to be okay and then the doc did what I told him to do and he was passable. Not good. Just passable.

I was waiting to get Lilly in for her MRI when Larry told me to fuck off. He didn't know that I hadn't slept in two days and I was sick to my stomach all day and my wife and I sat on the couch in the morning after we got Lilly off to school and cried for half an hour. He didn't know that even after she got the MRI Lilly still needed blood tests and it would be weeks before we would know anything conclusive about her gimpy walk and bum hand and whether she would live or die. It was just bad timing for Larry.

I STEWED FOR A DAY and then I made my plan. I had an old Colt Ace, a beautiful semiautomatic .22 that was built on Colt's classic .45 automatic frame. My old man gave it to me before he died. I loaded it with hollow points and drove to Larry's shop early and waited for him to open up. I watched him put his key in the lock and I got out of the car slowly and followed him into the store, closing the door behind me.

"Morning, Larry."

"Howyadoin' Will."

He was wearing his usual orange Hawaiian shirt and a puka shell necklace, and he wasn't happy to see me.

"I need my fucking money."

"Jesus, Will. I haven't been to the bank yet. I don't keep any money in the shop."

I took out the Colt and pointed it at him. It looked just like a .45 and Larry's knees buckled.

"For Christ sake, Will, whaddayadoin'. You know I'll pay you. You know I'm good for the money."

I shot him twice in the gut and he fell back on a nice little National lap steel amp and flopped a little bit. Then I put one in his head. The Ace had no recoil and it was pretty quiet—that was the beauty of a .22. And we were in fucking Escondido, so I didn't worry too much about a little noise. There was an amazing lack of emotion in the whole transaction. I didn't feel a grand sense of justice. I just felt that it was all necessary. I walked out of Lost Guitars, shut the door behind me with my elbow and got in my car.

I took the scenic route home. My general theory is that whenever you can drive on Coast Highway, you should always drive on coast highway. I stopped at Agua Hediondo Lagoon and the mullet were jumping and the beach was empty. I walked toward the inlet and threw the Ace in the lagoon as far as I could. It hurt me to get rid of that gun—my old man traded for it from his boss, who didn't know shit about guns. It was the only good thing my old man ever got out of his boss.

When I got home, Carol was at work and the kids were in school. I grabbed my Harmony Sovereign, a surfboard, a wet-suit, some camping gear and some clothes and threw it all in the back of the Land Cruiser.

GETTING ACROSS THE BORDER is the easy part. The Mexicans welcome gringos like me coming into their country to spend money. I make sure that I drive slowly through Tijuana so I don't get pulled over by any Federales. I have been rousted there many times, but I have always maintained it's simply the cost of doing business in Mexico. No hard feelings.

You have a short conversation, ideally in Spanish, ask them how much you need to pay, negotiate a little, give them a reasonable amount of cash and drive off.

I get on the toll road and head toward Rosarito. I know now that I'm not going to see my wife and kids for a while. I'll call Carol tonight and let her know that I'm in Mexico and I need to take a little break. I've done this before. She knows that I'm fucking burned out, and she has more patience with me than anyone on the planet. She doesn't know, however, that I killed a man today, and I don't intend on telling her anytime soon. And there's a good possibility that no one will ever know who killed Larry Olsen. He kept no records of our limited transactions and there were plenty of people who didn't like him and no path leads to me. Still, I start to rationalize. I have tried to be a good husband and a good father and a good son and a worker. I tried to show love to the people who I care about. Still, I have fucking failed. Miserably failed.

I see the sign for Tecate Jacks and decide to check out Baja Malibu. Sometimes you see turds floating in the water there, but it's a thumping, hollow beach break that's as good as any place on the West Coast when it's working. I see one of the parking attendants with his fake Federale shirt and badge.

"Hola. Buena tardes."

"Buenas tardes."

"Quiero estacionar aquí. Cúanto cuesta?"

"Cinco dolares."

I give him eight bucks to park and thank him.

"Tiene un buen dia."

"Igualmente."

I love that word *igualmente.* Equally. The same to you. It's one of the best words in the Spanish language. Maybe one of the best words in any language.

I walk down the cobblestone road to Baja Malibu and it's firing. Head-high, with A-frame tubes going off up and down the beach. I walk back to the car, put on my wetsuit and wax my board. I can smell the trash from the alleys as I make my way to the beach and walk through a pack of dogs looking for something to eat. A black alpha dog, part shepherd and part chow, growls at me.

"Vete, pinche perro." Get away from me, you fucking dog, I tell him. He senses there's something not right with me, and he leaves.

I'll surf until I get tired and then I'll drive down to K-58 and set up camp. I'll make a fire and cook a skirt steak over mesquite and make *tacos al carbon* with fresh flour tortillas and salsa. And then I'll open a bottle of good tequila, a nice *reposado*, and I'll drink shots and chase them with a *Negra Modelo,* and I'll pass out in the warm, narcotic Mexican night.

One Week in Oaxaca

THE LOVE OF MONEY will make a man do almost anything. That's what my friend in Oaxaca kept telling me and I believed him. He was sharpening a Buck folding knife, getting ready to cut off the bottom of my right earlobe. He told me to be still, that it would be nothing more than getting my ear pierced. Just a little prick, he said. But I did not believe him about that.

As Felipe dabbed my ear with a cotton ball soaked in tequila, I remembered a conversation with my uncle, who spent most of life as an oil rig worker in the desolate stretches of West Texas. Twenty-five years ago he talked to me about Mexico when my wife and I were getting ready to go on our honeymoon to Cozumel.

"I want you to do me a favor, Nate," he said. He was in his sixties with a full head of beautiful, wavy gray hair, and he wore a one-piece, lime-green work suit that men in Texas over forty put on pretty much every day they can. "I'm begging you not to go to Mexico. It's a helluva dangerous place and you might never come back."

I told him he was crazy, that Cozumel was perfectly safe. It was no different than going to Florida, but the food would be better and the people much more tolerable. I was right about Cozumel. Not so much about Oaxaca.

IT'S DAYBREAK and we are crashing through the last stretch of the dicey dirt road in a rental Jeep to get to a break called Punta Blanca. I have been coming here for about eight years now. James and I used a surf guide service the first few years and learned what we needed to know: the barely passable, muddy roads that lead to the point breaks, the names of the men who patrol the land and how much we would need to pay them, the right tides and wind patterns. My Spanish is well above average and making friends with the locals is about seventy-five percent of the game. You couldn't get to every break—the local guides controlled some of them exclusively. But you could get to enough uncrowded places that would make your whole weeklong trip and you could surf more empty, pumping waves than in a week than you could in three months in Southern California.

I see the point and it is perfection. James is too hungover to surf right away, so I have the place to myself this morning. I make the hard paddle out in the warm water and try to be patient, waiting for the best set waves. There may be a few locals or Americans who show up later in the morning; but now, for a couple of hours, we have it to ourselves. The sets line up on the point and I tend to take the third wave—just habit from when you surf with a crowd of horny expats who are always taking off on the first wave they see. The wave goes on for a hundred yards and you can get shacked a few times and come out and then you kick out and slowly paddle out to do it again. Occasionally I see dorado breaking the surface in the distance, and once, way off in the distance, I see whale spouts and get a glimpse of a fluke. This is everything that Mexico is supposed to be.

After two hours, I am dead tired and still haven't seen a soul other than James, who finally paddles out, and I get one last wave and make my way to shore. I see a 1970s Ram Charger and a Toyota pickup come out of the jungle and five Mexicans get out of the vehicles. The problem is they don't look like surfers. One guy in his twenties has his long-sleeve cowboy shirt half unbuttoned and I can see the Mayan sun tattooed on his chest. I walk toward him and start the conversation.

"Buenas días. Como estás?"

"Bien, bien."

"Hay olas esta mañana."

"Si, si. Pero para mi, las olas no estan importantes esta mañana."

That's when I know that I am fucked and I think about running. But where could I go? I am too far from shore to make it back to the water and the reality is I am terribly slow. I might have been able to run a six-second fifty on my best day thirty years ago, and the five Mexicans are wiry and fit and could run me down in a matter of seconds. And I think of the humiliation of running and getting caught from behind and getting my face slammed into the sand so I decide to just stay right where I am. James is walking toward me and he sees that I'm talking with the locals and probably thinks everything is all right. He speaks no Spanish other than *"Hola señor"* and *"Quiero una cerveza."* Neither one of those lines will help us now. People don't understand that the folks who work for the cartels and kidnap foolish Americans for a living are nothing like the slovenly bandits in the *Treasure of the Sierra Madre,* and that was a very bad thing for us.

JAMES AND I SAT IN A ROOM TOGETHER, handcuffed to heavy furniture, and admired each other's amputations. They had cut off his small right toe. These were unpleasant things for us, but they were just small statements to our families. A piece of an ear lobe. An ugly little toe. They would prompt emotions and move our loved ones to action, and action meant sending money.

I got to know our caretakers pretty well during the first week. Felipe was a nice looking kid in his early twenties; his English was very good and we talked about surfing the sand points in the area and the best tides. Julio, a gruff, thick man in his forties, was not as talkative and his English was poor. We knew that he liked to eat, and we spoke to him in Spanish about the local *mercados* and the best places to eat *chapulines*—spicy fried grasshoppers—and we couldn't get much more out of him.

Felipe explained the plan to us. He needed email addresses for our wives, and he would send pictures of us—highlighting the tight shots of the missing body parts that he took on his handy little iPhone—and work out a payment plan. These guys were plenty sophisticated—they understood technology and they had obscure email addresses that couldn't easily be traced, and even if someone did come up with a location in Oaxaca, it was meaningless. They moved us periodically from one dumpy little house to another and they owned the local police force. Americans underestimate the efficiency and the focus of the cartels. These are highly successful businessmen—they know their markets, they know how to make huge amounts of money and they want to diversify into any area where they can make more money. They're just like Exxon or Apple, but they don't have to spend nearly as much on marketing. The kidnapping business is not as profitable perhaps as the cocaine or marijuana business, but it still makes them plenty of money and it doesn't take a lot of personnel to get the job done.

And the cartels also know that there's was no way our wives could get the FBI or the DEA or anyone else to give a fuck about us and do something significant to find us. We were just middle-aged, middle-class adults who knew exactly what we were doing when we went to Oaxaca—we had read the tourist advisories and the government's warnings against traveling to the area and we went anyhow. We had no connections to high-ranking congressmen or law enforcement and we didn't make big donations to political causes. As far as the government response was concerned, the answer was simple—fuck your husbands or fathers or sons, they said to our families, only they said it in much more official, pleasant terms.

ON THURSDAY MORNING FELIPE CAME TO ME after he had sent the first email to my wife with the pics of my ear. He had a response and he wanted to make sure he was understanding things correctly.

"Nate, what is this I am reading from you wife? You did not tell me that you are sick."

"Well, you never asked."

He had printed out a letter that my wife attached in her response to him and put it in front of me. I knew what it said—I had written it. It went like this:

June 5, 2013

TO: The family, friends and attorney of Nathaniel Dixon

FROM: Nathaniel Dixon

SUBJECT: Travels to Mexico

I am writing this to all of you with a clear head and sense of purpose. You all know that my melanoma has metastasized to my bones and my liver. I still feel good enough that I'll likely take one more trip to Mexico before I die.

But here is my mandate. If I get abducted when I'm in Mexico, you will give the folks who take me nothing. I do not care what they say they will do to me or what they show you. I am a walking dead man and they cannot hurt me. Your only task is to send them this letter.

Thank you and I love you.

"*Pinche gringo.* So what are we to do now, Nate?"

"You need to do whatever you want next. I don't need my

earlobes or toes at this point. I might have three more months to live. No more than that. And my family will get my life insurance either way—if you kill me or if I die from cancer."

This was a difficult situation for my friend Felipe. The cartel had invested considerable time and effort in me, and they were looking for a return on their investment. Perhaps they could bring a doctor in to run some tests and confirm that I had metastatic stage 4 melanoma, but that would cost them even more money.

"So you think you can take it if we cut off your hands or your feet? You think that you won't start begging your family to send money?"

"I don't know if I can take it, Felipe. I'm pretty sure I won't be too brave. But you need to know that in addition to my letter, I've had long conversations with everyone in my family as well as my attorney, and I've made it very clear that they can't send any money to people like you. I have kids in college, a good life insurance policy and whatever money I have is going to my family. Your leverage in this whole game is that you can threaten to kill me and everyone on the planet knows that you will do that. The problem is I'm already dead. My family knows that all too well, and now you know that."

THEY LEFT JAMES AND ME IN THE SAME ROOM for the rest of the day, and we talked through things.

"It would have been nice to have one last uneventful trip to Oaxaca," I said.

"You know how it works, Nate. One of every four trips you get fucked in the rear. But this is the worst we've had."

"You know where I stand on this. They get nothing."

"I know, buddy. But you know that my family is going to pay. My prick father-in-law died six months ago and he had four houses in Laguna that he bought in the early 1960s. When Jane and her sister split up everything and sold the houses, they each came away with about seven million dollars. I don't know what I'm worth to her and the kids, but they will pay to get me out."

"I want you to get out. Nothing means more to me, my friend. But don't let them extort any money from you to pay for me. I'm not a good investment at this point in my life. Save the money for your kids. Maybe they can come down here to surf with you in a few years when things settle down."

"I'm not coming back any time soon."

We fell asleep in our sweat, leaning against a wall with tattered pictures of *Penthouse* centerfolds. I dreamed of paddling next to gray whales, seeing their spouts and an occasional fluke.

EARLY IN THE MORNING Felipe and Julio came to the room. They both look tired—they were over this whole mess.

"Nate, we're going for a drive," Felipe said. He put a blindfold on me, an old orange bandana that smelled like Mexican mud.

"Don't kill him, you motherfuckers. He's my friend." That's the last I heard from James.

They walked me outside and put me in the back of a vehicle that I figured was the Ram Charger. I could smell the gas from the carburetor when they fired it up and admired the throaty roar of the Dodge V-8. I can tell you one thing—it's not pleasant to drive in the backseat of a vehicle in rural Mexico with a blindfold on. I had tried to be detached with my "I'm already dead" mantra for the whole week; now, however, we were approaching the final move in this journey. My legs quivered uncontrollably and I felt like I was going to piss myself—I wasn't nearly as tough as I thought.

I bounced around in the back of the Ram Charger for a long time and my mind went to many places, none of them good. It was the same as you when you wake up at three in the morning and your little brain starts racing, trying desperately to figure out how you're going to pay for your kids' education, how you're going to tolerate your fucking job for another day, how you're going to listen to your ninety-year-old mother say that she can't remember things and she's lonely and why can't you come visit her more often. Although I'm a failure at yoga, I've tried to at least grasp the concept of breathing. I counted to ten, slowly inhaled and exhaled, and reached for some things that were enduring in my life. The clean smell of my wife in the morning. My son playing his acoustic guitar and singing a Mumford and Sons song. My daughter charging up a mountain as we hike a trail in the Eastern Sierras. At the same time, you think that at this point in your life you're ready. You always hear old people talk about how fast life is, how in a blink of an eye they were young, energetic and beautiful (they never were) and now they look and feel like hell every day—they can barely walk and their knees are shot and they can't breathe. I never bought that bullshit. Life is amazingly long, especially if you're a middle-aged man with a big mortgage, a wife and kids, a crazy old mother and a drug-addict sister all leaning on you each day. Life is an eternity when you can't find anyone around you to talk about *Candide* or *Absalom! Absalom!* or Curtis Mayfield or Cornell Dupree. You just have to listen to your fat neighbors drone about their new fucking lawn mowers and their shitty jobs and their loser kids.

The Ram Charger slowed and came to a stop and I braced

myself. Someone opened the door and and grabbed on to my shoulder like a vise and pushed me out of the car. My stomach churned and I thought I might puke. One of my captors pulled the bandana off my head and I saw that it was Felipe. I blinked for a moment and adjusted my eyes to the bright sun and looked to the ocean. It was Punta Blanca. It was surprisingly flat and nobody was out.

"We are done with you, Nate," Felipe said. Julio stood next to him and was disinterested in the whole affair.

They got back in the truck and Felipe stuck his head out the window.

"Que tengas una buena vida, Nate."

"Y tú, Felipe. Y tú."

I walked to the sea and jumped in the warm water. I stayed under for a good twenty seconds, popped my head up and saw the Ram Charger moving down the beach.

I sat on the sand for a while, moving my index finger over my left ear. I looked up at the relentless Mexican sun and slowly made my way to the road.

ACKNOWLEDGMENTS

A FEW YEARS AGO, an idea surfaced in my little head that I had been kicking around for more than 25 years. It was partly inspired by Sherwood Anderson, the great American writer of the early 20th century who had a profound influence on Ernest Hemingway and William Faulkner, among others. There's a story about Anderson that has taken on a life of its own. I wrote my graduate thesis on Anderson, so I know a little about him. The story—part legend, part fact like most good stories—goes that Anderson walked into his advertising business on a fall day in Chicago in 1912 (he was in his 30s) and realized that he wanted to be a writer and left and never went back.

I am not an impetuous man, but I always liked that story. And like Anderson, I thought I had at least one good book of short stories in me. So I talked with my enlightened wife and kids and pitched the idea of taking one year off work to write a book—a career sabbatical, if you will. I promised that I would live simply and not consume all of our savings for life and college. I told them that it would be an adventure, that it would be a time that we would remember for the rest of our lives, even if it meant that I would have to work until I was an old man. They didn't hesitate—they said go, they said jump, they said write the book you want to write. They only had one proviso—I would have to cook restaurant-quality meals for them every night. No problem, I said.

So this book is dedicated to Ann, Hank and Allee for encouraging me to jump and take an adventure that I'll never forget.

Along the way on the adventure, I had some other folks who encouraged me. My late mother, Alene, who grew up in the Depression and always worried about money, thought it would be a great idea for me to write a book and helped out with college funds for her grandchildren. My father, Dale, who passed away in 1999 on the same day Joe DiMaggio died, was always an inspiration and a great storyteller in his own right.

I want to thank my surfing buddy Jeff Lipscomb, who has been a mostly competent driver and guide during our trips to *Baja Norte* and *Baja Sur.* Fortunately, he lets me speak Spanish when we get into binds, and that has kept us out of Mexican jails at least a few times.

Ellen Slezak, Kevin Wilson and Steve Hawk read early

versions of some of the stories and told me to keep working. Michael Burge did a thorough and sympathetic job of copy-editing. James Teague made sure that my Spanish dialogue was grammatically correct. Susan Blettel designed the book and brought her elegant sensibility and attention to detail, as she made sure I pulled everything together. My old friend Marichal Gentry yelled at me from New Haven when I hit a wall and told me to finish the damned book.

You think when you finish a book that it's the end of something. But it's not. The stories live in your head and you think of better ways to tell them and new stories that need to be told.

ROBERT BRADFORD
Carlsbad, California
May 2015